FOR LOVE

&

INVISIBLE STRING

A MATCHMAKERS' BOOK CLUB NOVEL

NICOLE VIDAL

COPYRIGHT

Cover design by Ashlee Nassar of Designs with Sass
Developmental Edit by Katherine McIntyre of Hot Tree Editing
Final Edit by Sharron McKenzie of Hot Tree Editing

ISBN 978-1-961365-89-6

TABLE OF CONTENTS

KEEP IN TOUCH WITH NV

Facebook (http://fb.me/NicoleVidalAuthor)

Instagram (http://instagram.com/nicolevidal_author)

Amazon (https://www.amazon.com/Nicole-Vidal/e/B082DJHPXP?ref_=dbs_p_ebk_r00_abau_000000)

My website (www.nicolevidal.com)

Pinterest (http://pinterest.com/NicoleVidal_Author)

Goodreads (https://www.goodreads.com/author/show/19827329.Nicole_Vidal)

CHAPTER ONE

CARLY

I take my place at the front of the room and open our Matchmaker's Book Club meeting at the Hagen residence. They have a beautiful home with access to a large private yard on the outskirts of town.

"I would like to call this group to order. Welcome, ladies." I have been pondering my opinion and what to say since they attempted to set me up after our last meeting. The matchmakers are fun, but I don't want to be fixed up. Ironic, I know.

A slew of replies echo around the room. Eva Hagen, Maggie Washington, and Kelsey Ramirez are sitting in a tight circle off to my right with wine in hand. Lina Gugliotti and her sister, Lia, are huddled together on the white couch in the rustic living room.

Scarlett Smithson, one of my besties, barrels through the front door and takes a seat in the armchair to my left. She mouths an apology for her tardiness. "Sorry."

"Before we get started, I want to address your attempt at fixing me up." I look pointedly at Maggie. "I don't want to be the subject of your matchmaking. I will rebuff any attempt to find a suitable partner for me by this group. I love you all, but I don't want to find my better half due to your meddling." I hear the hypocrisy in my words. I want to find a man to spend my life with. I wouldn't mind if my group mates conjured the meet cute. It simply doesn't seem like the right man is out there for me, at least not in York Beach.

Maggie sits up straighter. "Each woman here is a testament to said interference. Our success rate is impeccable."

Undaunted, I reply, "That may be true, but pairing me with Séamus wasn't a match. The idea of a stranger photo shoot was interesting, but the subject should be exactly that… a stranger."

Kelsey is shaking her head. "We can't agree to taking you off the list of eligible women. You're a catch and deserve to be happy like the rest of us."

Technically, I'm not an honoree. I don't meet the eligibility criteria since we halted adding people to the list. At one point, we discussed including doctors and nurses but tabled it until we exhaust our current candidates. Kelsey means they could pair me with someone on the list. I want nothing more than to find a man for myself like these women have. I'm disappointed I haven't yet, quite honestly.

"I'm confident none of the nominees are going to work for me. I'm removing myself until we reach a point where we are adding to the pool again. Can we at least agree on that?" That is a lie. One of the men intrigues me, but history ruins any chance we may have as a couple.

Looking around the room, I see my book club buddies reluctantly conceding.

Maggie huffs, "Fine. We'll refrain from attempting to set you up until the list is reopened to new candidates."

"Thank you." Turning to my right, I say, "I would like to welcome Tatum Percy to our meeting."

She smiles. "I'm happy to be here. How does this work?" Tatum stepped into my shoes at the stranger photo shoot. She stole Séamus's heart between shutter clicks.

The other members laugh.

I share the origins of our group. "Initially, we started as a gaggle of nurses and EMTs to de-stress from the rigors of our profession with a book club and a girls' night in. There were four women at the beginning. Now, we have a membership of more than twice that. Over the years, this book club evolved into a girl gang of epic proportions. Not only do we host events for the local children's charities, but we keep tabs on the most eligible singles in our community. Our matchmaking book club was created in good fun, and the tradition has continued for the last seven years.

Along with the purpose of our group, the rules for inclusion on the list have evolved. Inclusion requires a few factors balanced against one another. First, an attractive package is a must. Candidates and admitted bachelors or bachelorettes must be a member of our first responder community, including police officers, firefighters, and EMTs. Most importantly, we attempt to maintain secrecy until after he or she has been legally wed. Now, I open the floor to all members to raise a motion."

Slowly, Kelsey Ramirez raises her hand. "I wouldn't call it a motion exactly. I have been approached by a few members of the community inquiring about the group. Two specifically asked if they were on the list as potential subjects of our... dating experiment. Their preference would be removal as an honoree."

Ouch!

Lina Gugliotti adds, "I had a similar experience. I won't name the person, but she wanted to be taken off the list. Her words were something like 'I have enough trouble with my family members trying to find me a husband. I don't want a group of women I barely know attempting it as well.'"

I can surmise it's likely a member of the YPD for Lina as her husband, Tino, serves as our community resource officer with Callan Craven.

"Yikes! I move to delete those three potential honorees?" My question is posed to the membership.

The ladies vote, and the motion to remove those who are disinterested is carried.

"Kelsey and Lina, please let me know who has requested to be taken off the list. We certainly don't want to force the issue."

Maggie Washington speaks up next with sadness laced in her words. "Are we looking at the end of our matchmaking endeavors?"

I frown. "I hope not, but if our friends and coworkers are completely against our efforts then... perhaps we should consider stopping that portion of our group." The matchmaking part of the group is fun but it wasn't the original intent. Our track record is exceptional, but if the community is against it, ending that endeavor makes sense.

A low hum of chatter begins.

"Why don't you talk amongst yourselves to come up with our next honoree? Until everyone begs off, I think we should continue."

Rather than wait for the end of the meeting, Kelsey and Lina join me near the front of the room.

"If we scratch those who don't want to be matched...," Lina looks directly at me, "then what is the point?"

"I understand your frustration. Which woman asked to be removed?"

"Piper Montgomery," Lina replies.

Kelsey adds, "Lacey Ransom and Callum Foster."

A sliver of hope passes through me. My brother is still an option. If we're nearing the end of our tenure, ideally, we can find him a partner first. The vote was close when Landry was suggested last time. "Very well. I'll strike those three. I don't love where this is going though."

Kelsey purses her lips. "Me neither. I'll share this disheartening news with Gladys and Lois." They were the founding members of our book club.

I walk around and hear names like Aidan Madden, Landry Reed, and Mia Arden. I gaze out the large window in the direction of the shore. After about ten minutes, I meander through the chatting ladies and retake my spot at the front of the room.

"I open the floor to suggestions."

Eva Hagen raises her hand. "Have we paired two people from the list to each other?"

I tap my lip with my finger. "No, I don't think so. Anyone recall?"

The consensus is we haven't.

"Who are you suggesting?" I ask her.

"Landry and Mia. Both are YFD. Mia is a little younger, but given your overshare about his social life, her age could be a benefit," she replies. Eva's right. Chances are Mia isn't up on the town rumor mill and it could be a blessing for my big brother.

"You have a point. Any objections or additional recommendations?"

I pause to give them a chance to voice concerns. Hearing nothing, I state, "I'll reach out to anyone uniquely situated to assist in matching Landry and Mia. Before we get to this month's book, I want to remind everyone about the softball tournament preparations. Our group is the main organizer this year. We need to secure at least two fields and set up merchandise, as well as snacks. YPD has offered Hagen to assist. The EMT liaison is Lacey Ransom. I'm waiting on the YFD helper."

"Don't forget shirts and trophies," Lia Blake adds. She joined our group after falling for Finn, a newer member of the YPD.

"The trophy is currently housed at the police department. It goes to the winner of our events each year. We do need shirts though," I reply.

"I'll share the current honoree list. How it may change is yet to be determined. Please vote on your way out if you want to continue with our matchmaking endeavors or focus more on the book club and philanthropy aspects. Currently our list of potential honorees includes the following from the York Police Department: Donovan Davis, Xander Greyson, and Esmeralda Garcia. York Fire Department includes Bradford Collings, Alden Rhodes, Aidan Madden, Landry Reed, Kellen McCormick, and Mia Arden.

Lastly, the EMTs in York County include Jude Pascal, Hollis Booker, Marcello Auberon, and Tobin Vaughn."

The ladies start clamoring over this month's book. *The 24th Hour* was written by James Patterson and Maxine Paetro. The novel features a Women's Murder Club. Scarlett thought it would be a fitting read and departure from our usual romance picks.

As much as I would like to continue our group, perhaps it's time to cease meddling in the affairs of others. Our level of success is unheard of. I see all sides, but stopping means no more happy couples and that's disheartening. I refuse to tally the vote to end our search of happily ever afters for our first responder community, at least for now. If we stop matchmaking, it might save me from my friends meddling in my love life again

CHAPTER TWO

ALDEN

The busy months of the year are rapidly approaching. My small town on the Maine shore is fantastic. The tourist traffic begins to increase in late March or early April. We are on the cusp of the former right now.

I was raised here and can't imagine living anywhere else. York Beach is a quaint seaside location with a stately lighthouse, a cobblestone-lined street with shops, and even an amusement park. Nearby there are plenty of things to see and do, including state parks and outlet malls.

"You wanted to see me, Cap," I state, knocking on his office door. Calling my father's former lieutenant, twin, and my uncle by his title isn't foreign like it was at the beginning of my career. Stephon Rhodes is younger than my father by three minutes. My only saving grace is they were fraternal not identical twins. If they were, working side by side nearly daily would've been harder after losing my dad a few years ago. The death of a parent is expected. It doesn't compare to losing Asha and our baby girl by a wide margin despite it occurring even longer ago

"Please have a seat." He points to the chair across from him. "I'm putting in my papers for retirement. I've had a great run in this office, but the demands of the job are taking a toll on me."

"Congrats?" My response matches the lack of conviction of his statement.

He laughs heartily. "It's that obvious, huh?"

"That you may not be ready to quit? Yeah, it is."

"Either way, I want you to take over for me. I've spoken with Chief Bertoni, and he's in agreement."

Whoa! Running this house would be a dream come true. At least I'll accomplish one good thing in my life. I push my stray thoughts away. Since losing my family, positives are viewed with skepticism and concern. I learned the hard way. The best things don't always stay. Usually, I'm able to keep my thoughts in check while I'm on the clock. "Me?"

"You earned your seat in this chair." He stacks books on the edge of his desk. "These are the manuals for the YFD. You should study them with special attention to the forms at the end of the binder. Your test results from the last exam are still valid. Otherwise, the promotion requires a vote from me and the chief."

I remind myself there's still time for me to have a family although it's an outside one. Thirty-six, single, no kids, and a steady, heroic job is more than enough for most women. The problem isn't the ladies. It's me. I have been out of the dating game for too long. Plus, I forgot a single huge descriptor that every woman in town sees when they look at me… widower.

I had a fairytale courtship. Asha and I started dating in high school and never looked back. We met freshman year at the first pep rally. The school recognized each member of the sports teams. She was a cheerleader. I was the only swimmer from York High, which put me at the back of the line. Asha was the tallest, which meant she was beside me through the introductions of every other fall and winter athlete.

Just before they called my name, I stepped closer to her and whispered, "Will you share a pizza with me this weekend?"

As Alden Rhodes reverberated around the gym, she shouted, "Yes. I'll meet you in the quad after school to plan."

I looked over my shoulder and flashed my signature dimpled grin in her direction. Then, I waved to my schoolmates while walking across the stage.

"Alden?" My uncle's voice pulls me out of my head.

"Yes. Thank you for the opportunity. You won't regret it."

He shakes his head. "I know. Please keep this to yourself until I file my retirement packet."

"Will do." I rise from the chair and extend my hand to him. Instead, we hug, and I leave his office. I wasn't expecting to inherit this house so soon. I'm excited for the opportunity. I don't have much time before the alarm sounds and we're off to a call.

I grab my gear and slide into the passenger seat of the engine.

"Reed! Hustle up!" I shout before closing the door.

Landry is an above-average firefighter once he's locked in. However, he often lacks urgency to get to an emergent situation.

I use the radio as he leaves the station. "Engine Four responding to 1400 Watercliff Terrace."

"Roger. Additional units en route for backup," Craig from dispatch states.

Reed enters the complex and maneuvers the large engine to the rear of the community. Numerous high-end townhouses are set around a man-made lake.

The homeowner is standing on her porch waving furiously. "Oh, thank goodness! There's a fire in my kitchen. I tried to put it out, but the extinguisher didn't spray." The woman is a tiny thing with salt-and-pepper hair. If I had to guess, she's probably in her late seventies.

"Thank you, ma'am. Reed and Madden, make entry and assess. Foster and McCormick, prepare a hose line to the lake."

"Copy, Lieutenant," Madden answers. Aidan Madden is from the same recruiting class as Reed. They are opposite in nearly every way. Madden's neat and always on time. Reed is not. How they pull off being roommates is beyond me. Reed grabs a hand extinguisher before following Madden inside.

A few minutes later, they return to the rig. "Fire is out. It's contained to the stove area," Reed states. Turning to the woman, he says, "Ma'am. You'll need to get that stove serviced by a professional or replace it."

She throws her arms around Reed and exclaims, "Thank you, young man. I lost track of my dinner. With all that's happening in the world, I was distracted by the newscast."

"You're welcome," he answers. Then he steps away to assist Foster and McCormick in rolling up the hose.

Shortly after arriving at the station, my shift ends. I turn in for the night. Tomorrow morning, I'll have a few hours before family dinner. Plenty of time to shower and change.

Previously, these meals felt like forced torture. As mightily as I try to get out of it, dinner with my sister and mother is requested and required at least once a month. The unavoidable family time started about six months after I lost my family in an accident. The get-togethers grew less frequent until after my dad passed away a few years ago. The time with my family has grown on me significantly. I look forward to it now.

I drive the short distance to my mother's house and park behind an unfamiliar car in her driveway. Knocking on the door, I wait for it to swing open.

"Uncle Alden!" My nephew Halston greets me with our secret handshake. He's eight years old and the spitting image of his dad.

"Hey, bud. Whose car is that?"

"Grandma's boyfriend."

I frown. "Thanks." *Boyfriend?* Mom would've told us about him. Right? Following Halston, I hug my sister, Essie, and her younger son Henry, who tops out at five. Then I raise my eyes in question.

She whispers, "I didn't know either."

"Has Mom mentioned he was her boyfriend?" Attributing that word to a man in my mother's life is difficult. Before my dad's death, my parents were married for forty years.

"She didn't correct Halston. It must be accurate," Essie replies. My sister is two years younger than me. She's tall and thin with mocha skin a shade darker than mine. "Ready for this?"

No. If my mom can date again, shouldn't I be able to do the same? When I consider acknowledging my interest in a woman other than my wife, betrayal makes my chest tighten as if it were in a vise. True, I fulfilled my end of "until death do us part," but moving on hasn't come easily for me. I tried dating about two years after I lost Asha, but it was excruciating. Weeding through the locals hoping they didn't know my story beforehand, was step one. If they didn't, the small talk was simply too much. After a few months of failed dates—two to be exact—I conceded a local "need not apply." Considering I didn't intend on leaving York Beach, bachelor life became my new plan. "Nope. Who is it?"

"Harvey Kingman," Essie answers.

He's a local and spends time with my mom and Evelyn Penn. If I recall correctly, the three of them have each been through the loss of their spouse.

"There you are." My mother crosses the kitchen and hugs me.

"Hi, Mom." Before releasing her, I notice a bouquet of flowers on the counter. I turn to him and offer, "Mr. Kingman, nice to see you."

"Good evening, Alden. You as well. Please call me Harvey."

I nod and take a seat while he greets Essie. "Where's the hubby?"

Essie smiles. Her husband, Halston Jones Sr, is the mayor of our fair town. "He's preparing for a committee meeting."

My mother sets food in the center of the table. Silently, we dig into her unmatched lasagna, salad, and garlic bread. Gladys Rhodes can cook like no one else. When I was competing, she would make sure healthy food was available for me. During my college years, she would send meals weekly to my apartment. I studied fire science at the University of Cincinnati. It was a four-year program that allowed me to swim competitively as well.

There was no grand announcement regarding mom's dating status other than Halston's statement. However, she seems happy, and for that I'm grateful. As I watch my mother and her companion interact, I reconsider my life alone. Has enough time passed? Can I jump back into the dating game? Honestly, there can't be many women left in town who know my story and are single. I would still lean toward ignorance at this point.

I escape to my quiet home on the outskirts of town shortly after dessert. Soon after we married, Asha and I bought a fixer-upper. It was a disaster, but it was affordable and in a great neighborhood. Most importantly, it was ours. The old adage, "buy the worst house on the best block," would be an apt description. We didn't require a lot back then, but we hoped to have a large family. Asha wanted a massive walk-in closet with space to dress, and I needed a pool. Back then, I wasn't training for anything specific, but I swam daily. Still do.

I lost myself in rehabbing the house for a few years. I started with a four-bedroom colonial with an office and an unfinished walk-out basement. Now, I have a modern home with a main floor master suite, including Asha's closet and a finished game room in the basement. We were still in the planning stages for the nursery. I'm grateful. Tearing it down would have broken my heart again. After making our kitchen usable, I built an inground heated pool. Unfortunately, it only bought me about three extra months before I had to close the pool for winter. Two years later, I built a structure over it allowing me to swim year-round. It's kind of a marvel. I'm able to retract the sides during the warmer months. Completely worth the money.

Once I arrive home, I drop the mail on the island and immediately prepare for a swim. I pad out the back door and enter the pool from the deep end with the perfect dive. My events were solo during my competitive carer. These days the laps are my therapy. I met with a lovely doctor after I lost my wife and daughter. Talking wasn't enough for me. I still found my way into the water frequently. I stopped the appointments and focused my intentions while in the water about a year later.

Each lap I think about something different. First, I admit an attribute my beautiful late wife possessed. The next, I focus on a dream I had for our unborn daughter. Third, I find a positive aspect of my day. Fourth, I ponder a way to improve tomorrow whether in my profession or my personal life. This is where I typically get stuck and end up swimming miles and miles in the pool before exhaustion takes over.

Today is a bit different than past years. My thoughts float to dinner with my mom and Mr. Kingman. While my father wasn't stolen from us, the effect is the same. He's gone. Gladys Rhodes deserves to move on. A new companion and card partner makes sense.

If finding someone to share life with is acceptable for my mom, why isn't it for me?

Content I won't find an answer with more laps or even tonight, I exit the pool and return to the house. This time though, I give myself a deadline to dip my toes back into the dating game. I'll bring a plus one to the First In, Last Out Ball, no matter what. Six months should be long enough. Right? I'm not convinced.

CHAPTER THREE

CARLY

Hectic is the only way to describe this morning. I shouldn't be surprised. It's par for the course in the York Memorial Emergency Department. I'm the supervising nurse. The title means I handle the schedule and oversight of the floor. You would think my job would make me grumpy or grim. On occasion, like two days ago when a young girl came in with a gruesome injury from the playground at school, I leave here not in the best mood. More often than not, my outlook is pleasant and cheerful.

Today has brought a steady stream of patients, including a couple of hikers who got lost near Mount Agamenticus. For a tourist, I can see it happening. There are numerous trails, and with the spring heat, it makes sense for them to lose their bearings. Hagen and his K-9, Roxy, found them a few hours ago.

The upside to being in charge is I have an office. It allows me to handle paperwork and such in private and quiet. Around noon, I escape the floor and hunker down before my brother is set to arrive for lunch.

"Hey, sis." Landry announces his presence without knocking.

Not shocking. My older brother does things on his terms and in his own time. He always has.

"Did you bring it?"

He smirks at me. "Perhaps."

"Seriously though. You had one job, Lan."

He laughs deeply. "I completed my task. Your turkey sub topped by banana peppers plus oil and vinegar. I brought sour cream and onion chips and a raspberry iced tea from Vocaturra's, madam." Landry sets the bag on my desk.

"You're my favorite brother."

Landry scoffs. "Stiff competition there. I'm your only brother."

"Still makes you number one." My brother and I get along well. While he's older, I took on the stereotypical caretaker role. The skills dovetail nicely with my profession. I'm happy we were able to have lunch,

"Funny. To what do I owe the pleasure of your company? You never invite me to have lunch without an ulterior motive."

"Ouch! True, but damn!"

Landry laughs. "Spill it, sister."

"I'm volunteering you to be the YFD liaison for the softball game."

He grouses a little bit and takes a bite of his own sandwich. "What exactly does it entail? I don't have a lot of spare minutes on my hands with work."

I glare at him. He can't be that busy. He's a firefighter in our fair town. His schedule is set. He works forty-eight hours and then has ninety-six hours off.

"Don't give me that look. How do you have time to spearhead the event yourself?"

"I have less than you, but I enjoy my philanthropic endeavors."

"Stop with the big words. I'll help, I guess."

"Best ever!" I shove a few chips into my mouth and wash them down with the tea. "I need you to rally support, draft a team, and garner donations."

He grumbles. "Fine. When is the game?"

"Yay! Thank you. I'll be sure to include you when we have our next meeting. We're still nailing down the exact date. The hope is late June. The funds raised are for Craven's college assistance endeavor and a scholarship at York High." Callan Craven is the school resource officer and created a few great programs during his tenure. This one offers help to students with their entrance essays like peer review and editing and application fees in exchange for community service.

"Speaking of meetings...."

I frown at him.

My brother continues, "I know you and your gaggle of book club friends selected me for your next target."

How? Who is the leak? A wave of nausea quickly passes over me. Do our fellow first responders truly dislike the premise of the group?

"I've been seeing someone. I don't plan on sharing who, but I need you to stop whatever is planned for me."

My head shakes involuntarily. "What are you talking about?"

"Don't play dumb, Carly. It's beneath you. The first responders in our community don't want to be your pawns anymore. Your list is no longer a secret, and we're done." I guess Lina and Kelsey were right.

"Who told you about the honorees?"

"So you admit it?"

I purse my lips and reply, "No."

"You've had a successful run for the last seven years or so. Your meddling needs to stop." Landry crosses his arms over his chest.

A wave of sadness ripples through me. I understand a few people wanting to be removed, but for the most part, the group is unintrusive with our methods. "I can't take you off a list if there isn't one. You're going to have to spill the beans about where your information came from."

Is it worth it anymore? We deleted three at our last meeting. Now my brother wants off. *Ugh!* I spearhead this group mostly for the comradery with the members and the charity events. We would be fine with only those tasks—at least I believe we could be.

"The same way you're protecting your group, I will for my source. I'm dating someone and don't want to be fixed up. Okay?"

I close my eyes and process his words. We aren't in the business of breaking up relationships. "I can neither confirm nor deny that you may or may not have been selected. However, I'll pass along your request not to be fixed up at this time. I won't remove you from the alleged list given your poor track record in selecting women to date."

"Whatever. I gotta go." He seems dejected that I won't simply agree to leave him alone. I don't fully trust him to find a good partner on his own. Oher people in town, perhaps, but not Landry,

"I'll text you when the next meeting for the game will be."

He waves me off and exits my office in a huff.

That went well. At least I achieved my short-term goal of volunteering him to help me. I don't have long to consider my options before I return to the emergency room. The afternoon will feel short considering I have a staffing meeting at four with the hospital administrator.

Once I leave my office, I watch three ambulances come and go for a multicar accident near the center of town. The only good news is the injuries were relatively minor for every passenger.

With my mind still reeling from lunch with my brother, I take the elevator upstairs.

My meeting with Willa is at a set time each month. We go over the current staffing levels and discuss if changes are necessary or improvements can be made. I knock, but she doesn't answer. I can hear talking in her office. Before I opt to walk in, the door swings open.

"Hi, Carly," Luca Cappelli states. He and Willa have been married for nearly five years. They have two adorable kids with a third on the way. They met by chance or through Luca's persistence, depending on who is telling the story. Later they learned her father was his training officer before he returned home to York Beach. He has since moved to a position with the State Police.

I clear my throat and eye his disheveled uniform. Luca guffaws, fixes the collar, and tucks the tail of his shirt.

"Luca. Have a nice evening." I look past him at Willa, who is bright red with embarrassment. She's gorgeous. Her jet-black hair is shiny from the pregnancy. They don't know the gender, but given her complexion and hair, I'm thinking it's a boy.

"You too," he replies. After a glance back at his wife, he rushes away.

Willa states, "I'm sorry."

I raise my hand to stop her. "No need. If I were lucky enough to have a man in my life, I would take whatever time I could get, especially with our demanding professions."

Willa is my bestie on top of being my boss. Well, more like a coworker. "Perhaps you should let our friends set you up."

I can speak freely, as she's part of the group but hasn't been able to attend meetings lately. "The list doesn't have anyone I'm interested in."

"I know you know I know you're lying," she quips.

Willa is one of two people who are aware of my previous interest in one member of the YFD. Previous isn't true. Dating him requires dredging up a day I wish to forget. He's closed off. "It isn't a lie. He is perpetually single. and therefore is unavailable. I know better than anyone to not pursue men who are disinterested."

My friend shakes her head. "That was different. Kenneth lied to you. It isn't the same thing. There were no indications he was married when he took the position here. Not even a telltale tan line on his ring finger. You never would've dated him if he were truthful."

"You're right."

"Of course I am. Nothing says you can't put yourself out on a limb and ask Alden on a date despite your traditional girl preferences."

Willa is right. I want an old-fashioned romance, complete with manners, flowers, and honest conversation. My parents' relationship isn't one I want to emulate. I have enough examples from my friends and their parents to witness a solid marriage. Mr. and Mrs. Cappelli, Luca's mom and dad, have been married for north of forty years at this point. I suppose some of the novels we read provide examples as well. Does romantic fiction ever come to life? Yes. Really? Doubtful.

"I'll consider it." I open my file, and we discuss my staffing plans. Putting myself on the line for Alden hasn't crossed my mind. His choice to remain single speaks volumes.

After I lay out the details, Willa responds, "That works for me. I appreciate you. Please think about what I said. You deserve to find the happiness you have given numerous couples from our group."

"Thanks." I've learned the hard way not to go back down to the ER after these end of day meetings. More than once, I was pulled into a call or employee drama. I want none of that tonight. Returning to my office, I place a carryout order at Barley and Hops and exit to the parking lot.

The brewery has been open for the last few years of so. Recently, the owner expanded their menu to include entrees. They have artisan beers on tap and the best fajitas in town. I'm not one to eat at a restaurant alone. At home though is not unusual.

"Hey, Carly." Jimmy, the owner, greets me from behind the bar.

"Evening."

"I'll grab your dinner. Be right back."

I nod and look around the dining area. Seamus and his fiancée, Tatum, wave. They are joined by Zara, Tatum's younger sister, and her boyfriend, James Cavallaro. The younger couple are star runners at the high school.

The only other patrons are Piper Montgomery of the YPD and the guy she's speaking with. He's obscured by her frame. She transferred here from Florida. She's older than me by a few years. She shifts on her stool and her conversation companion is revealed. Alden.

In my mind, I give him the once-over. The man is tall, lean and has perfect mocha skin. The dimples in his cheeks are sexy too. His physique was honed from a young age and hours upon hours in a swimming pool. There is no question, the man is hot as hell. He's a lieutenant with the YFD and a bona fide local.

I overhear him say, "I'll see you then," as he returns her phone.

"Good evening, Carly," he says as he approaches the opposite side of the shiny oak bar.

"Hello, Alden." I mutter as he walks to the exit.

Jimmy returns and hands over my dinner.

"Thanks," I mumble and leave as well. The ride home is short. In no time, I'm catching up on old episodes of *Sweet Magnolias* before the new season is released, while I wolf down my dinner.

The good news is I don't have to pay close attention. I've seen these before. My mind wanders through the events of the day. I harumph about Landry begging off because he's dating someone. We'll see how long that lasts. My confidence in Landry selecting a partner isn't high given his track record. I land on Alden.

I have so many questions. Is he dating Piper? For how long? Did I miss my chance? That would suck. Then again, I haven't made my attraction to him known in any way. Willa's guidance to ask him out was solid. The reality of taking it requires dealing with a horrible day in the past for both of us.

CHAPTER FOUR

ALDEN

Many questions drift through my mind as I push the water away during my laps. This morning is particularly focused though. Over the years, I have been attracted to a woman here or there. I simply never acknowledged the feelings or pursued them. Over the last week, my action items have been to accept my feelings toward a member of the opposite sex. The key for me is to remind myself that I'm not betraying Asha by moving on with my life. Frankly, if she could speak to me now, she would pitch a fit about my lack of a partner seven years after losing her.

My nerves are off the charts. I'm scheduled to have a coffee date with Piper in a few hours. On the surface she's attractive and has a steady job with the YPD. I know almost nothing about her. I'm aware she isn't a local, which is a huge plus. Piper has no information regarding my relationship history. I'm looking forward to a date without the word "widower" stamped on my forehead.

Other than the laps in the pool, I have my sister and Rafael to talk to about Asha. Stepping back into dating requires speaking with Rafael first, then Essie. My sister will share with our mom the instant our call ends. I met Rafael at a grief support group. We've been friends ever since. He lost his partner of ten years to cancer a month before Asha and our daughter were stolen from me.

I climb the stairs at the edge of the pool and towel off. As I walk into the house, I thumb out a message.

Me: Tell me this is the right thing to do.

Rafael: It's time.

Me: Says the newlywed.

I attended their wedding a few months ago. Rafael and Mauro had an intimate ceremony on Long Sands Beach.

Rafael: I was you for a shorter period.

Me: I'm trying.

Rafael: I know. The first one is always the hardest.

Me: Thanks, man!

Rafael: I expect a full report.

Me: Maybe.

After downing a protein drink, I shower and stand in Asha's closet, staring at my wardrobe. It's a space she never got to use. I have nothing to wear on a date. I shake my head and opt for jeans and a running hoodie. It's just coffee. I keep repeating that statement. Perhaps the pit in my stomach will dissipate rather than swallow me whole.

Once dressed, I grab my keys and drive to The Perk. It's a *Friends*-themed coffee shop. There are pictures from the show as well as memorabilia on the walls. The owner is Kelsey Ramirez. She's married to YPD captain, William Ramirez. They have two adorable kids, Valentina and Benjamin.

You can do this. It's just coffee. I grab the handle of the café door and pull it open. Each action seems harder than normal. The door is heavier, and my feet weigh a ton as I walk. With my wife, our interactions were light and easy. We were excellent at communication.

The eatery is bustling with people. It's surprising, considering we haven't reached peak tourist season. Also, it's early morning by weekend standards. I glanced around and note Piper hasn't arrived yet.

"Your usual today, Lieutenant?" Becca behind the counter asks. Becca is the manager and has a rolodex of coffee and pastry orders for repeat customers in her head.

"Yes, and one of Kelsey's scones of the day."

"You got it."

I shift to the pick-up area. My foot is tapping subconsciously while I wait for my order and my date. She's late. Not a great start. With my breakfast in hand, I take a seat along the front window. I can see a sliver of Short Sands Beach from here. Well, it's more the ocean, but either way it's pretty.

I'm halfway through my pastry when Piper bursts through the door.

She looks right and then left. "Alden. I'm so sorry for my tardiness. My son...."

I offer a greeting after an extended pause. "Morning."

"The reason isn't important. Thank you for waiting."

Her son doesn't rank higher than a coffee date. "You're welcome. Would you care for a coffee?"

"No thanks." She takes a seat across from me.

"Your son?"

"Did I not mention him? He's seventeen and made some poor choices last night."

"If you need to deal with that, I understand."

She shakes her head. "He's fine for now. I slept through my alarm. You're YFD, right?"

When I decided to date again, I tried to find a woman who wasn't local. Piper is the only one I know that fits my criteria. She's slightly older than me and a transplant from Miami. Her height rivals mine, and she's in shape. Not surprising. I'm sure the physical standards for police officers are similar to ours at YFD.

"Yes, I've been with the department since I graduated from college. You relocated a few years ago, right?"

"We lived in Miami until three years ago," she replies.

While her exterior is pretty, the vibe is off. I can't put my finger on it, but even when I was ignoring my attraction to women, I felt something. Not with her. "How do you like it here?"

Her attention is drawn away from me to the other patrons. "Sorry. The people are nicer, but the weather isn't great. I had beautiful sunshine almost daily at home. The winter months are drab and boring. Also, there's nothing to do. My hometown is bustling with activity and interesting people."

Inwardly, I bristle at her response. I heard her words but also the implication of the same. She likes clubbing, dancing, and fancy restaurants. Good for her. Not something I'm interested in. I repeat Rafael's words in my mind: *The first one is always the hardest.* I press on. "Do you have any hobbies?"

"Not really. I mostly go to work and take care of Kyle. He wasn't happy when we moved here and frankly still isn't. His father joined us as well but returned home recently."

Not calling where you live home isn't a good sign. "Is he looking at colleges?"

Piper isn't paying attention to me anymore. It's likely she didn't even hear my question. I lean back in the chair and sit in silence. I watch the clock across the room tick for nearly three minutes before she asks.

"What did you say?"

Done. I push my chair back and stand. "It was nice to meet you, but your mind is clearly elsewhere. Have a great day."

"Can we meet for dinner, maybe at Morgan's?" she asks. The restaurant is higher end and run by its namesake, August Morgan. He and his wife Caroline are newer additions to the community. If I recall correctly, she works with her sister-in-law Noelle at the daycare and writes children's books.

"I don't think that's a good idea."

"What's wrong with you? I'm a catch." Her question is forced out at high volume and with attitude.

A hush falls over the patrons in the coffee shop. All eyes are focused on us. *Hell no.* I take a step closer to her and whisper, "You may be for someone else. Have a nice afternoon." I nod tightly and exit the door on the street side.

Apparently, I wasn't clear. Piper is beside me as I cross to the parking lot. "Seriously, I would like an answer."

I pinch the bridge of my nose and decide disclosure will work. "You were late and not paying attention at all. More than once, you were distracted by the people in the store."

"I'm a cop."

"I know, and that's why I let the first instance go. However, the second time was for slightly more than three minutes."

"You timed it?" Her tone is incredulous.

"The clock was above your head. Thank you for coming, but it's best we part ways here."

She puts her hand on her hip and adds, "Fine. You aren't my type anyway."

Without an answer, I continue toward my car. Instead of leaving, I walk along the shore of the beach and take a seat on a bench, allowing the soothing sounds of the waves to help dissipate my feelings a bit. Why say yes to the date if she wasn't attracted to me? Makes no sense. If she wasn't planning on getting to know me by paying attention, why show up?

I drag my hand down my face and watch the waves roll in. You would think I would avoid the area where my family died. Initially I tried, but it's impossible.

An hour later, I drive home. I'm not scheduled to work until tomorrow morning at seven. My schedule is forty-eight hours on and then ninety-six hours off. There have been some rumblings about changing to a different system, but I don't think it'll happen. I certainly won't approve a new schedule when my promotion is official.

Rather than jump into the pool again, I pull out the manuals Cap provided and skim the pages. Most of this isn't new information. I slow down when I reach the higher-level forms and directives. In the late afternoon, my phone chimes. It's likely Rafael checking in.

I'm surprised when I see Landry's name in the notifications. Landry is one of my subordinates. He's a solid firefighter and a decent guy outside of the house.

Landry: Are you on shift tomorrow?

Me: Yeah. Why?

Landry: We can talk then about the softball game.

Me: Sounds good.

Each year, the York Beach first responder community hosts a charity sporting event to raise funds for the resource officers in our school system. Last year it was a 5K. I finish my reading and prepare an early dinner. Only when I sit to eat does Rafael call. I answer, despite the probability of my meal turning cold.

"Hey, man! How did it go?"

I exhale slowly. "Not great, but I did it."

"Proud of you, man. How are you feeling?"

Hiding my true emotions won't get me anywhere with Rafael. He knows me well. "Slightly dejected. Ready to throw in the towel and stay a bachelor forever."

"You don't truly want that, do you?"

I reply, "No. Nothing has changed. My desires are the same... a partner and a few kids to guide through life."

I can hear empathy in his response. "You know bringing Asha back isn't possible. Try again, my friend. Mauro was my third date after Elio lost his cancer battle."

"I felt like I was on a roller coaster. At the beginning of my date, I'm at the top of the hill. After careening down the slope—today at least—I went completely off the rails rather than making it back to the start."

"I understand."

I pull my lips into a tight line. "I know you do. Thanks for calling. Beers soon?"

"Sure. I hope you cancel on us though because you found someone prettier to spend your time with."

Me too. "From your lips, my friend." I take a bite of my chicken and rice stir-fry. Luckily, it's still warm enough. Once I finish eating, I consider more laps. Instead, I finish the books Cap provided before turning in early.

CHAPTER FIVE

GLADYS

It's been quite some time since I've been in the thick of the book club happenings. I've had two unexpected conversations today about the group I founded many years ago.

During my morning walk on the rail trail near the beach, I ran into Kelsey and her adorable children. The converted rail trail is a three-mile loop.

"Gladys, it's wonderful to see you."

"You as well, dear." I greet her son and daughter too. "Aren't you both the sweetest?"

Valentina offers me a little wave. Ben shoves his toy car in my direction. I would estimate Ben is about five and his sweet sister is three.

"Do you have a moment to chat?"

I frown but reply, "Of course, dear. Old ladies like me have nothing but time."

Kelsey smirks. "You aren't old, Gladys. You're experienced in life."

"You're too kind. I like it though. How can I help you?"

She explains the uproar from members of our first responder community and those requesting removal from our list.

"Oh dear. That's sad."

Kelsey offers her kiddos some crackers while we sit. "I agree. Our success record is unheard of. We have removed those who requested it and selected a new honoree. However, we wanted to make you aware. The members hope we aren't nearing the end of our tenure, but our outlook isn't promising."

"I suppose all good things must conclude at some point," I offer. The matchmakers have had a longer run than I anticipated. In fact, we never planned on meddling in the personal lives of our fellow first responders. It happened accidentally with the Mitchells. Micah is a nurse at York Memorial, and his wife Jodi was a member of the YPD. We paired them for one of our first community charity events as cochairs. They fell in love, married, and have four children. Micah now works as a home health aide, and Jodi is a dispatcher in a nearby town. Once we realized our book club was uniquely situated to foster love matches, we gently guided our friends and coworkers toward solid relationships.

Kelsey shrugs. Ben spills the crackers on the ground, and Valentina starts crying. "I appreciate your time. Carly asked me to give you a heads-up."

I continue my morning walk and ponder the likely demise of at least the coupling part of my girl group. I resolve to come up with some kind of solution in the coming days.

When I arrive home, I have an unexpected visitor camped out on my front porch.

"Hello, Mama Rhodes." Landry greets me with the moniker the members of the YFD gave me. I often drop off meals and assist in our community outreach at the firehouse.

"Is my son okay?"

He immediately reaches out and takes my hand. "There is no need for alarm. Alden is fine. Well, he was last time I saw him at the station. I'm here with a request for myself."

"Very well. Would you like to come in?"

"Thank you," he replies and holds open my screen door.

My late husband and I bought this large cape about six months after our wedding. It has a large wraparound porch and a good-sized yard. I refuse to move. Alden and Essie can decide what they want to do with the family home when the time comes. For now, I close off the upstairs to cut down on costs and cleaning. "Would you like a drink?"

"Sweet tea if you have it," he replies.

I laugh softly. "You know better, young man."

Landry winks at me. "Yes, ma'am."

With two glasses poured, we take seats at the oval kitchen table. "How can I help?"

He draws his lips into a tight line and begins. "I have tried talking to my sister, but I was unsuccessful. I'm aware of the matchmaking aspect of your book club."

When I'm nervous or feeling exposed, I wring my hands, so I lower them beneath the table. "I see."

"A trusted source shared that I'm the current honoree being fixed up. The issue is I'm dating someone. My sister refused to remove me from the list but agreed not to meddle for now. She doesn't trust my taste in women."

"Oh. I'm sorry. You want me to convince Carly to remove you?"

He drops his head and answers, "Yes, please. Mia is different from my previous girlfriends. We started off slowly, and I can't allow anything to mess it up."

"How long have you been dating Mia?"

"Six months." His answer is forthright and unwavering. He's telling the truth.

"Yet, you haven't introduced her to your sister." My tone is accusatory on purpose. "Why not?"

"No. Given our family history, I decided to move at a glacial pace. Carly is sometimes a lot to handle, despite being my younger sister. She's fiercely protective and wants the best for me. I'm aware and grateful. Carly would've never selected Mia for me."

Interestingly, that is precisely who the group paired. Mia Arden is also a member of the YFD. She's a little younger but an excellent match for Landry. This meeting, along with the probable demise of our matchmaking endeavors, presents an immediate solution.

Putting it into play requires assistance from an unlikely conspirator, Landry himself.

"I have a suggestion."

"What do you have in mind?"

I share my plan and what I need him to do to help me pull it off. If pairing our first responder community is coming to an end, I'm going to pull out all the stops to join the two most reluctant but perfect-for-each-other first responders in my last act as a founding member.

CHAPTER SIX

CARLY

A few days have passed since lunch with my brother. I have considered my choices as the leader of the book club. Plus, I was in charge of facilitating Landry's match. He wasn't lying about dating someone. I'm sad he didn't feel like I should meet this woman. It makes me even more interested in figuring out who she is.

I considered calling an emergency meeting to select a new candidate, but it doesn't seem necessary. Given the state of our honoree list, we need to create a new approach or consider ending our Cupid ways completely. I reached out to Kelsey Ramirez and Alannah Craven to share the information that Landry has opted out of our meddling because he's in a relationship. Both expressed a desire to hold off until our next meeting to choose a new honoree. Reluctantly, I agreed. My concern is holding off will expedite the demise of our group.

I focus on my job and dealing with the staffing issues. Deena, one of my newer hires, has shared her pregnancy has become high-risk. She's been put on bedrest. The schedule I prepared with Willa took a hit, but I amended it successfully. Within a few hours, Scott, one of my APRN's, offered his resignation. His wife works for a technology firm whose headquarters is relocating from Boston to California. The only plus is I have two weeks to amend care team levels. The final straw for today was a letter slipped under the door of my office.

It isn't ominous as far as my safety, but it is for keeping my job. My nurses and support staff are demanding wage increases and more personal time. They have given me a thirty-day deadline to come up with a plan or they intend to unionize. *Great!*

I take a few deep breaths and call Willa.

"Hey, Carly. What's up?"

I explain the letter and set up a meeting with her to discuss my options and if there's any room in the hospital budget to meet their demands. After the morning I've had, I spend my lunch hour upstairs on the pediatric floor.

While I thrive in the chaos of the emergency department, I have always wanted to be a NICU nurse. It's my dream job, in fact. Our facilities here are top-notch. Our survival rate is one of the highest in the country. There hasn't been an opening here in years. Our current staff is phenomenal and have no plans to move on. Maybe someday. In the meantime, I cuddle and bestow love on the preemies and help out where I can in a caregiving capacity.

I use my badge and enter the locked area of the hospital.

Scarlett Smithson waves from behind the glass. She worked for Zack, caring for his mom until she passed. Sadness casts over me when I recall they were one of the first couples paired under my tenure with the matchmakers. She's a few years younger than me, but her family life made her savvy. We became fast friends when she started working here. She's my go-to person when the local celebrities and athletes want to visit the kids.

Scarlett is discreet and doesn't fangirl over the likes of Marco Cappelli or Cian Fleming, who both play professional soccer. Even when Ellis Barnett or his costar Demi Goldberg learned of a sick child who was a huge fan, I called on Scarlett to be involved in the planning and execution to keep the press at bay.

I gown up and take a seat in one of the cushioned rockers.

"Rough day?" Scarlett asks.

I nod as she places a preemie in my arms. Johan was born at thirty weeks. He's nearing his time for discharge. Most preemies reside in the pediatric NICU until close to their original due date. In this little guy's case, he has about two more weeks before he's ready to go home.

Scarlett maneuvers the wires and tubes. Then she asks, "Want to talk about it?"

I look left, then right, and reply, "Yeah, but not here. Wine at my place tonight?"

"Sounds good. Does six work?" she asks.

"Perfect. I'll grab our faves on my way home." I absorb some baby cuddles and try to forget about my crappy day. I'm only slightly successful.

The remainder of my work day passes, and I find myself walking out of the liquor store with more wine than Scarlett and I can drink tonight. Good thing wine is meant to stay in the bottle to age.

I stop next door at the family-owned Italian restaurant and pick up a carryout order. The last thing I want to do is drink on an empty stomach or cook for that matter. I arrive home and change out of my scrubs. As I walk downstairs, Scarlett rings my doorbell.

"Come in," I shout, and she enters my house. Both of my besties have a key.

"Wow! You changed already too?"

I nod and search for a corkscrew. Losing my scrubs is a must for me as soon as I'm in for the evening.

"What's up, sweetie?" she asks while setting down her purse and hoodie near the door.

I tear the wrapper from the top of the bottle and pop the cork before answering my her. "So many things." I share with her about Landry and the book club as well as the letter from the staff. She knows about the latter, as her name was attached to it.

"Yeah, sorry for no heads-up on that."

I wave her off before handing her a glass of wine. We have strict friendship and professional lines between us.

We sit in my living room and chat over delicious lasagna and cheesy garlic bread.

"I'm sad that our group might be ending. You're more upset about not knowing who she is, aren't you?"

"Of course. I may be the younger sibling, but he stinks at dating."

Scarlett opens her mouth to speak but pauses. She thinks better of it and adds, "Pot meet kettle."

I take a heavy sip of my Haute Cabrière pinot noir. "It isn't that I don't want to date. I need a transplant. I can't date a local. We see too much. We know too much."

"You know and I know there is a local you would love to date, but you're a chicken."

I frown at her. "Am I though? Until recently, he hasn't been out with anyone. Plus, you're aware of my reason for not pursuing him. I'm sure he feels the same way I do about my presence on that awful day."

Scarlett swirls the wine in her glass but doesn't drink. "You can't be sure."

"Maybe I don't, but admitting to pining for years isn't a good look either."

Scarlett laughs. "Nothing wrong with it if the timing wasn't right."

I consider her words. She isn't wrong. "I did see him with Piper last week."

"Really?"

I nod. "I was surprised too. She's not a local though. It makes sense for him to date her. Piper has no clue about his wife and unborn daughter. She likely sees a sexy man in his mid-thirties with no baggage to speak of. She's wrong, but nonetheless." Then I realized she still hasn't taken a sip of wine. "Are you pregnant?" I blurt.

"Possibly, but please don't say anything to anyone. I haven't confirmed or told my husband."

"Were you trying?"

My sweet friend smiles. "Zack and I stopped actively preventing a pregnancy."

I lean over and hug her. "I'm crazy happy for you. I'm sure Savi will be excited that Emme and Ben will have more cousins." Savi is her older sister and married to Sam Morgan. They run an international insurance company. Numerous cousins are running around from Sam's brothers, Cash and August, as well.

"She will be. Mum's the word though." Scarlett hands me her glass. It'll save me a trip to the kitchen for a refill.

I pretend to zip my lips. "Want something else?"

"No, thanks. Back to you, maybe consider asking him out for coffee or something."

If he's dating again, now might be a good time. Perhaps it's best to leave the past where it belongs.

"I'll think about it."

"You should. Both of you deserve to be happy."

"Thanks."

We chat about the demands of the workers. I don't foresee being able to offer a pay raise as high as the ten dollars per hour they're seeking. Maybe I can spread it over a year or five but certainly not an immediate bump. Additional personal time is easier to add. That aspect of their request is more manageable. They are looking for two more days. The bigger question is what they're willing to offer me to get those things. Truthfully, there isn't much left to give on either side. The emergency department budget is stretched thin as it is.

"Between besties, if you can make any headway with the demands, you should be good. I'm sure the requests are higher than what the workers would settle for."

"I appreciate you."

"Same."

"What is your plan for Landry?"

I exhale slowly. "If he wants to keep this relationship private, even from me, I can't stop him. I wish it weren't the case. Hopefully… eventually, my brother will trust me enough to share the identity of his girlfriend."

"I'm proud of you, Car," Scarlett offers.

"Thanks. Our parents were awful examples of relationships with each other as well as with their new partners now. I don't want to smother Landry, just be in his corner." My parents divorced when we were in our teens. Both moved onto second marriages. Our stepmother stays at home with her dogs and spends insane money on beauty treatments. Our second stepfather is a drunk, and we don't speak to him or our mother now.

Scarlett smiles widely. "You need to tell Landry that word for word."

"I will."

She gathers her dishes and sets them on the island. "I'll see you tomorrow. Maybe you can come hang out with Johan again or Haven."

"We'll see. I'm supposed to meet with Willa beforehand. I don't foresee an hour being enough time."

"Fair point." We hug, and she leaves. After I clean our dishes, I grab my phone and charger and snuggle into my bed. I decided to heed Scarlett's advice and text my brother.

Me: I don't want to smother you and your girlfriend.

Me: I just want to be in your corner.

Surprisingly, he answers immediately.

Landry: I appreciate that. This relationship feels different, and I'm protective, is all. I'll think about an introduction. Love you, sis.

Me: I'm happy for you. Love you, bro.

It's progress, I suppose. After reading a few articles to keep up with advancements in my field, I grab some sleep. Tomorrow will be a stressful day.

CHAPTER SEVEN

ALDEN

The last few shifts have been pleasantly quiet except for Landry's request yesterday.

He asked me to step in for him as the YFD liaison for the planning committee. His sister is in charge of the charity softball game this year. She voluntold him. Landry begged me to take his place. Something about not seeing eye to eye with Carly about his love life and refusing to allow her group to fix him up.

Initially, I agreed because my mother founded that group, and I don't want it to end. They have been successful over the years. My position as his boss provides access to human resource filings in the fire department. We're required to disclose interpersonal relationships in the same house and under the same command. Landry has been dating one of his coworkers for a while now. I won't dig deeper into why Carly doesn't know who she is or the reasons behind it. It isn't my place.

After my usual swim and day-off errands, I drive over to Carly's to help her plan. I'm not even sure what she needs. Landry was sketchy with the details.

My disastrous date with Piper soured my interest in getting back out there a bit. However, I'm about to put my resolve to the test. While I haven't pursued a woman until recently, it doesn't mean I don't find this one attractive. She's smart and sexy as hell. Carly is a blonde bombshell. Her height belies her curves. The tiny package is intriguing. Physically, she's the polar opposite of Asha. Truthfully, there's only one reason I avoided her and my simmering desire to date her.

We went to high school together. Carly, like many of our classmates, watched my relationship with Asha grow and succeed. Two couples from our class are still together to this day. She's an OG local. If I recall correctly, we attended the same preschool as well. Then again, there was only one option back in the day.

I inhale deeply and take in her front porch. It's perfectly arranged with small lighted trees and a simple yet elegant welcome mat in a seasonal blue along with a matching wreath. Two Adirondack chairs with a side table are off to the right. With a knock on her front door, I settle my nerves as best I can.

"Alden? Hi." Carly opens her front door and greets me. She's wearing leggings and a zip-up over a fitted tank. Her feet are bare, and her toenail polish is bright red. She certainly wasn't expecting me on the other side of the door.

"You looked perplexed," I admit.

She purses her lips, and I'm struck by how sexy it is. How alluring she is in comfy clothes. "You aren't my brother."

Hell no, I'm not. I wonder what her outfit would have been if she was expecting me. "Landry asked me to step in and assist you with the planning.

Something about no time and future something or other. He was supposed to give you a heads-up too."

"Oh." She frowns. "Where are my manners? Please come in." As I pass her, she closes the door and tugs up on the zipper. *Damn!* The glimpse of cleavage was inviting.

Her home is cozy. It's a cape-style house set at the end of a cul-de-sac. Her décor appears warm and comfortable. A stab of missing a woman's touch in my own space washes over me. I don't have plush blankets or textured pillows on my couch. In fact, there aren't any in my house. I guess it's why Carly's feels welcoming and mine doesn't. "Your home is lovely."

"Thank you. Would you like a drink? I have water, iced tea, and flavored seltzer."

"A water would be great."

I accept the beverage, and we sit at her kitchen island.

"What exactly did my brother tell you?" Her hand is on her hip, and the hint of annoyance in her tone is cute. I'm glad her displeasure isn't aimed at me.

With a grin, I reply, "He didn't share anything other than what I stated. I'm willing to help."

She shakes her head, and the slight attitude with my presence melts away. Carly slides two huge binders between us. "Thankfully, we have a requirements chart from when Craven set up the flag football game. The basics are the same."

Notes of vanilla and maybe jasmine waft around me. It's intoxicating. Perhaps choosing to stay away from her physically was a wise decision.

That was before. I refocus on the pages in front of me as well as my intention to date again. It certainly isn't a hardship to spend time with Carly.

She sets forth the items that are already complete. "I have secured a few fields. I would prefer to use the high school, but the rec plex offers more space in one location."

"Playing in the same park makes sense to foster the sense of community. It decreases the overall length of the tournament as well."

Carly nods. As she does, a curly wisp of hair falls into front of her face. Without hesitation or thought, I tuck it behind her ear. I don't miss the goose bumps rising on her skin and the sharp intake of breath.

Carly meets my gaze and holds it. It could be ten seconds or ten minutes. I don't know or care. I'm mesmerized by her striking pale-blue eyes.

The tension zipping back and forth is unlike anything I've ever felt before. *Not even with Asha.* I swallow that last thought down hard. Silently, I remind myself my feelings and desires are completely normal.

She clears her throat and points to the second item on the list. "Lacey has agreed to set up the medical response and the first-aid area. Hagen will handle the security, T-shirts, and team draft." Lachlan Hagen is a YPD K-9 officer. I'm pretty sure he was set up by the matchmakers as well.

"Great start. Are you opening the volunteer hours to the high school seniors again?"

"It's a good idea and helps them earn their community service in a fun way," she replies.

"I can do that for you. I'll coordinate with Gugliotti," I offer and reach out to grab my water. At the same time, Carly turns the page of the binder. My hand on top of hers sends heated sparks up my arm.

"Alden...."

The pause makes me think she's going to send me packing. Carly must feel the same tension. Right?

She continues but not in the way I'd hoped. "Thank you," Carly replies instead of addressing the jolt of electricity between us

I'm not sure if she resolves not to touch me again or if it happened unintentionally. However, we reach the last page of the checklist. My to-do list grew a little, but it's manageable. I made notes in my phone rather than writing it out.

"Is there another sheet?" I ask.

She laughs softly. It's sweet and infectious like her. You would think her profession would make her hard and callous. Not Carly. She's cheerful, bubbly, and refreshing to be around. "No. We're set for now." Carly pushes her stool away and slides to the hardwood floor, which is the perfect shade of gray to coordinate with her décor.

I follow suit and stand as well. "Oh, great. When will we meet again?"

We both move toward the door and bump into each other at the corner of her massive granite island. I stop and urge her to go first.

"Does two weeks work for you?" she suggests when she turns to look at me.

I would be lying if I said I wasn't checking her out from behind. Her hips would fit perfectly in my hands. I shoved my desire toward women down. My attraction to Carly is too strong to suppress that task.

"For the game, sure." I will my heartrate to slow decrease and ask, "Have dinner with me?"

"Like a date?"

"Yes." My response low and laced with concern she might turn me down.

"I don't think that's a good idea." Her expression is completely neutral. There's no indication that she felt the heat between us earlier.

Old me would simply leave it at that and move on. Instead, I ask, "Did I imagine the tension and chemistry whizzing between us? The heat when I touched your hand?"

"Not at all." A stroke of crimson flushes her flawless face.

I steel my resolve and press forward. "Why not?"

Despite her decline of my invitation, Carly eliminates most of the space between us. I'm not sure if it's to support my fall from her answer or a genuine desire to be closer to me. I'm secretly hoping for the latter.

She looks up at me, and the kindness staring back at me is difficult to bear. "I was there." Her eyelids flutter closed, and she turns away from me.

I reach out and cup her elbow before walking around to face her again. "I remember. Every detail is etched into my mind from the moment I answered my phone to the moment I buried my wife and daughter." Talking about my family has gotten easier over the years. Most people don't ask anymore. My fault for secluding myself in my home aside from work.

Heavy silence hangs in the air around us. She's looking anywhere except directly at me. I wait nearly a minute to lift her chin with my hand before adding, "I resolved recently that one day in the past shouldn't control my future anymore."

She exhales slowly. "Are you sure?"

I draw my lips into a tight line. "I've studied every report I could get my hands on. You did everything in your power to save my family."

A single tear rolls down her cheek. She quickly wipes the trail away. "I failed." Her concern for my reaction inexplicably intrigues me.

"You know as well as I do my wife was gone before she reached York Memorial." I can't resist any longer. I circle her with my arms and draw her against me. Her small but curvy frame molds perfectly to mine.

From the information I gleaned, Asha was traveling along the road near Short Sands Beach. It was raining heavily, and the road was puddled with standing water. My wife slowed nearly to a stop after she rounded the corner. An inexperienced driver careened too fast around the curve and hit her from behind. Asha's vehicle slammed head-on into a telephone pole near the playground. Unfortunately, another car struck Asha's, and they hydroplaned down the small hill. She was trapped for nearly an hour before extrication.

Looking back, I'm grateful I wasn't on shift that night. My father and uncle prevented me from going to the accident scene. I waited for the ambulance to arrive at York Memorial with my family beside me. Over the years, I've made a point to think about that day and feel the anger, pain, and heartbreak. It's one of the reasons I stepped away from people who couldn't understand. The sullen and drawn expressions on the faces of the EMTs told me everything I needed to know. The outlook was bleak. I learned later they were considering whether they could save our daughter, not my wife. Asha was in her nineteenth week of pregnancy. Back then, the earliest born preemie to survive was born at twenty-one weeks.

Carly shifts and looks up at me. "Are you sure?"

"About moving forward? Yes. About you? Absolutely."

"Yes," she replies. One small word holding huge potential.

I smile and release her. That hug was the first time in years a woman has been that close to me. I didn't realize how much I missed physical touch until I drew Carly into my arms.

"When is your next day off?" she asks.

"Sunday," I reply.

"Okay. What is your number?" She reaches into her pocket and hands me her unlocked phone.

I add my number and text myself. "I'll plan our date and reach out in the morning." The words tumble from my lips, and I don't have the urge to hurl. This one will be different from the last.

She rises on her toes and kisses my cheek. "Good night, Alden." Unfamiliar sensations have been spiraling around my heart since I walked through her front door.

"Sweet dreams, Carly." I twist the knob and exit onto her porch. I wait until the lock is engaged before walking back to my SUV. Leaving here tonight with a date to plan wasn't a thought in my mind. Putting myself out there so soon after the debacle with Piper wasn't easy either.

I'm glad I did.

CHAPTER EIGHT

CARLY

First thing the next morning, I relive my meeting with Alden. That isn't accurate. It's been hours. All I can think about is how my heart nearly exploded when he tucked that strand of hair behind my ear. He barely touched me, and I was reeling. Then when he held me before he left... that was perfection. There's no other manner to describe how well we fit.

The sole reason I never pursued him was my presence on the worst day of his life. It doesn't... didn't seem right to divulge my feelings after a tragic loss. The more time passed, the deeper Alden retreated into solitude. I can't imagine the magnitude of a loss like he's endured. It took me years on the job to learn that I'm not a higher-powered being. I can't save every patient. Losing Asha and their daughter was my first loss in the emergency department. Now, looking back, experience has garnered clarity in the face of reality. Modern medicine can't save everyone, despite first responders working tireless to try to prevent death.

I agreed to a date with Alden. I repeat that phrase again in my head a few times. Only Scarlett and Willa know the degree of my pining for that sexy-as-hell man, and it shall stay in the bonds of besties. I resist the urge to call them this early in the morning.

I'm still in bed myself. Instead, I open our group chat.

Me: I have a date with Alden.

Willa: Yessss!

Scarlett: It's way too early... happy for you.

Her tiredness may be a symptom of pregnancy. I'm excited for her and Zack.

Willa: How did this come about?

Me: He showed up in Landry's place for the game meeting.

I keep the sexual tension to myself. It was magical.

Me: Then he asked me on a date before leaving.

Willa: Yay! No freaking out allowed.

Scarlett: ^^^^^ What she said.

Willa: When? Where?

Me: Sunday and I don't know yet.

Scarlett: He's planning?

Me: Yes.

Willa: Awwww.

Scarlett loves my reply, causing hearts to dance on my screen.

Scarlett: Why can't I love your answer more than once. There must be someone who can make that happen.

Me: I love you both the mostest.

Scarlett: Same.

Willa: Ditto.

Me: Have a good day.

Both like my message. Part of me wants to keep this development to myself for a little while. I believe he wants to move forward. I hope Alden feels the same when the time comes to show up. Clearly, his date with Piper didn't go well. That offers me a sliver of hope he'll come through. I throw back the covers and get ready for my day. It isn't going to be pretty, but the clock is ticking on the staff requests.

I scroll through my messages while my coffee brews. I'm pleasantly surprised to see a message from Alden. I smile at the formal way he input his name.

Alden M. Rhodes: Good morning.

Me: Hi. What does the M stand for?

While I wait for a response, I consider what to change his name to in my contact list. Should I disguise it for a little while? Instead, I amend my notification settings to private.

Alden M. Rhodes: Marcus. Do you have a middle name?

Me: Elisabeth.

Alden M. Rhodes: Have a great day. I'll call you when I can.

Me: You too.

I smile, fill my travel mug, and head to work. Today could go one of two ways: awkward or pleasant. I hope for the second option. It's been less than twenty-four hours, and I have a meeting scheduled to see if I can meet the staff demands. The harsh reality of the budget is a different story.

I greet Janie and Mikel at reception before stowing my bag. By the time I reach the nurse's station, an incoming trauma is announced.

"Multicar accident. Two adults for check, minor child with serious injuries, and an elderly patient with loss of consciousness."

"Mik, prep Bay One for the critical patient. Janie, handle the parents and child in Two. It's probably safe to assume they were in the same car."

The ambulance bay doors burst open. Penn and Lacey barrel through with the child, and the parents hustle closely behind.

"Bay Two." I direct them.

The doors don't close before Pascal and Vaughn escort the elderly patient inside. "Bay One."

My staff takes over, and I walk back and forth between the rooms to check on the status.

Then I overhear the information for Bay One. "Lois Canter, age 74. Loss of consciousness on scene. Laceration to forehead."

I didn't recognize her at first. She founded the book club with Gladys Rhodes. I hover near the entrance while my staff manages her care. Pulling myself away, I turn my attention to the minor child. Janie is prepping him for transport for an X-ray on his arm. His parents appear physically fine and more concerned about their son.

I step into the room and direct one of them to follow Janie with their son. The mom complies, and Dad sits in the waiting room.

"He's in good hands," I offer.

"Thank you."

Apparently, bad news travels fast. Gladys is standing near reception.

I walk over to her and greet her.

"Hi, Gladys."

"How is Lois? I'm her emergency contact."

I update her with the details I know. Gladys was a nurse here for twenty years.

"Thank you, dear."

"You're welcome. When they finish their workup, I'll have them come get you."

"How is the planning going for the softball game?" Gladys inquires.

"Good. I've delegated some of the remaining tasks to YPD and YFD. We're moving along well."

"Wonderful. I look forward to these events each year."

I smile and agree, "Me too. Please excuse me." As I walk away, I swear a sly grin grows on her face. I ignore it and review my notes for my meeting with Willa.

Before I head upstairs for my meeting with my notes and lunch in hand, the boy has returned from radiology. Janie works with him on the perfect cast color. In the elevator, I check my messages.

Alden M. Rhodes: Just a heads-up, Mama Rhodes is heading to the ER.

Me: Are we being discreet for a bit?

Alden M. Rhodes: I have no position one way or the other. She's a bloodhound though.

Me: Lol. I saw her and carefully answered her question about the game. No sharing involved.

Alden M. Rhodes: We can talk about it more later.

Me: Okay.

I exit the elevator and knock on Willa's door.

"Come in, Carly."

I comply and take a seat. "I would like to say I looked at the numbers, but I don't need to. I can't meet their demands without a bigger budget."

Willa drops her head in acknowledgment. "I know. We're going to have to get creative, or you'll need to cut staff to give the rest what they want."

"Scott resigned, so that allows me some wiggle room if I don't replace him. Breanna and Jolie will expect—rightfully so—a pay raise if the two of them are handling the work of three. It isn't enough."

Willa agrees. "I set up a meeting with the board of directors to ask for more money. Maybe they will allow me to reallocate some of the rainy-day fund. If they don't, we'll certainly be facing some gloomy days. Can you figure out the bottom line to give them a six-dollar bump over three or four years and one day of personal time?"

"Yeah, we will. Sure. When is your meeting?"

"Tuesday afternoon." She leans back in her chair and drops the stack of papers on her desk. "How is planning going?"

"Pretty good." I update her on the progress. Then my mind wanders back to my date.

"Earth to Carly? Are you by chance thinking about Alden?"

Crap! No. "Sorry, just worried about this situation we find ourselves in now." *Liar.*

"Me too." She bought it.

I bid her farewell and disappear into my office to eat my lunch. The good news is my afternoon passes quietly. That isn't a phrase you say aloud in a hospital or restaurant until the shift is over. Never. I grab my tote and exit toward the parking structure.

When I approach my front door, I notice a bouquet of flowers on the stoop. Warmth rises from my toes to my nose. It's been a long time since I've received flowers. Plucking out the small envelope, I read the handwritten card.

CER,

    I hope these brighten your day.

                AMR

I can't stop my stupid grin from him using our middle initials. The grouping is hand-tied and has blooms in hues of pink, purple, and orange, plus fun foliage. I lift them and inhale the sweet scent and smile widely.

Once inside, I change and then search for a vase. I find one after emptying the entire contents of my cabinet above my refrigerator. Before starting dinner, I send a text to Alden.

Me: Thank you for the flowers. They're beautiful.

I don't receive an immediate answer and prepare my food. Firecracker chicken stir-fry is quick and easy. I'm curled up on the couch with *The Night Agent* playing on my television. I prefer reading over watching, but I've recently been in a book slump. However, Gabriel Basso, the actor who plays Peter Sutherland, is easy on the eyes.

A flash of Alden passes through my mind. He beats the blond American actor hands down. While both men are real, only Alden is actually available for me to date. I imagined Alden to be a perfect specimen of honed muscle. When he held me, his entire frame was taut and hard. The ripples of his abdomen against me were exceptional. His racing heart was soothing despite our topic of conversation.

My inability to help Asha and their daughter was one of the hardest days of my life. I suppose we have that in common. Undoubtedly, Alden's was worse, losing his wife and child. Like him, I studied those reports. I dissected the actions of every single first responder that day. With therapy and a whole lot of self-reflection, I've accepted the reality. I did my best in a horrible situation. Now, I'm faced with reconciling that while dating the man himself.

My phone chimes with a text.

Alden M. Rhodes: You're welcome. Are you home?

Me: Yes. Just finished eating. You?

His name appears on my screen.

"Hi."

"I'm not a big fan of texting," he admits.

For my girls, texts are fine. For a man I'm getting to know, calls are better. "Same, actually. How is your shift going?"

He laughs quietly. "You know as well as I do. We don't comment until it's over." Like me in the emergency room, if he says it was slow, that will change in an instant.

"Understood. The grapevine is buzzing about your promotion. Congrats."
I heard about it today when Gladys arrived at the emergency room.

"Much appreciated. Cap is looking to retire. He has prepared me well. I took the exam last year for the opening at the house across town. Uncle Stephon wasn't happy about it. He feels like a Rhodes man should head up Station 25 in perpetuity."

"Was there another Rhodes before your uncle?"

"My grandfather also ran my station and his father before that."

"That's an amazing legacy."

"It is."

If I'm not mistaken, I hear despair and a note of longing in his short answer. Completely understandable if he was looking to have a houseful of children. The words tumble from my mouth before I can stop them. "I'm sorry."

I assume he'll thank me and move on from this topic, but he doesn't. His answer is unexpected. "I still have time."

My heart tightens. Alden wants a family even after losing his. From what I've seen with his extended family and our coworkers' children, he will be an exceptional father.

"Carly?" he calls after an extended period.

"I'm here."

"My answer shocked you into silence, huh?"

I tug my lower lip between my teeth. "Maybe a little."

"I am a father. I don't think the title is lost for me because my daughter didn't survive. I never had the ability to share my superpowers or hard-earned lessons with my little girl. It's an opportunity I would like a second or third or fourth time in my life. You don't want kids?"

"We're starting in the deep end."

"You don't have to answer," he states.

"It isn't that. I would like to have children, probably two. My age and my upbringing concern me though."

"You're in your early thirties, right?"

"Yes. The older a woman gets, the higher the risk for complications. Thirty-five is consider a geriatric pregnancy."

"A horrible term."

I chuckle at his response and share my reasoning for taking things slowly. "My parents are nothing like yours. Mama Rhodes is amazing. Your dad was as well. They were partners in every sense of the word. My mother is searching for her third husband while spending her second husband's money. My father is divorcing my stepmom as we speak."

Now it's his turn to contemplate his answer.

"Alden?" Nervousness creeps into my mind. Would a piss-poor relationship with my parents make him run given his stellar one with his family?

"I'm here. Working out my reply." He waits another moment and adds, "Your parents' failed relationships are examples of what you don't want. If you're honest about what you desire, then a lasting marriage is absolutely possible."

Cue the swoon. He wants to remarry and have more kids. "Thank you. I want a partner, not a roommate with a ring and tax advantages."

He laughs heartily. "That's a great place to start."

"I guess."

Our discussions so far are definitely not pre-first-date material, but I guess it's good to know where we stand.

"Do you have any issues with me planning our date?" he asks, switching topics.

While I'm not opposed to digging into my desires a bit more, I'm equally fine with the reprieve. "Fine with me."

"Any restrictions?"

"Like what?"

I can hear the smile on his face in his reply. "Do you hate dirt or water? Sports of any kind?"

"I don't hate dirt or water. An outdoor date would be fine with me. Sports are definitely on the table. I have a pretty good arm, or at least I did, if you might recall."

A hearty laugh comes through the phone. "I remember Miss All-Division and All-State Pitcher."

"Well, your accolades from high school significantly surpass mine."

"I did all right."

"Pu-lease. You were an All-American for three years in a row. I bet you still swim daily."

"Fine. I was pretty good. I do."

"One of the best is closer to accurate," I state.

"Thanks." Our call is cut short by the tones in the firehouse. "I gotta go. I'll call you tomorrow with the details of our date. Good night, Carly."

"Talk to you tomorrow. Be safe, Alden."

"Always."

I stare at my phone until the screen goes black. His acceptance of my presence on that fateful day was a huge push for me to be open to us as a couple. Butterflies flutter in my belly for the first time in years. It doesn't mean I'm still not terrified we may be perfect together.

CHAPTER NINE

ALDEN

As soon as I return to the firehouse, I text Carly. It isn't lost on me that even before our first date, I want her to be sure I'm okay. This event was long and arduous. The structure was located at the industrial park on the outskirts of town. It was thirty percent engulfed upon arrival. The call came in from a night security guard at shift change. Unfortunately, budget cuts decreased the staff. The guard started his rounds on the opposite side of the complex. It's a large area for one person to cover. Two of my crew were sent to York Memorial for minor injuries.

Me: I'm back at the station. I'll call you later.

I don't expect an answer. It's the wee hours of the morning. I hope Carly is peacefully sleeping in her bed. The thought hits me like a freight train. The blonde beauty is wrapping herself around my heart without even trying. I think about her when we're apart.

"Yo, Lieutenant." Landry taps his knuckles on the doorframe of my office.

The mere fact his sister was on my mind jabs me in the chest especially considering I know who he's dating due to their declaration of relationship. A tidbit of information that may come to bite me in the ass at a later time if Carly and I are as good together as I think we could be. "What's up?"

"I wanted to see how the planning was going with Carly. She's like the Gestapo when focused on a task."

No, she isn't. She's detail oriented and organized. "It's fine. I wouldn't characterize your sister like that either."

His eyebrows raise in keen interest. "How would you describe her?"

Internally, my radar is spiking. She's whip-smart, stunning, and carries her lost patients in her heart every single day, including my wife and daughter. I barely have words to describe her for myself. I'm certainly not ready to admit my attraction fully just yet. Never mind divulging my thoughts to Landry. "She was fine and normal. I don't know what you're getting at."

"So the meeting went well?" The volume of his voice increases as he asks.

"Yes. I have my action items, and we're meeting again about the game next week, I think."

He nods tightly. "Okay. Thanks for replacing me. I appreciate it immensely."

"You're welcome." I bristled while I agreed to meet with Carly in his stead originally. After one meeting and a date tomorrow, I may be thanking him profusely for helping me find a path to my future.

He turns and leaves without another word. Weird. Landry is the gossip of this house. A notification pulls my attention to my phone.

Rafael: Free for dinner soon?

Me: No.

Rafael: Details please?

Me: I have another date.

Rafael: At least you put yourself out there again and soon. Good for you.

Me: Thank you.

Rafael: Have fun. If it goes well, I would like to meet her.

Me: Sure. I'll let you know.

As I send that message, a response from Carly pops up on the screen.

Carly: Good morning. Thank you.

Me: You're welcome. I'll call you later with info for tomorrow.

Carly: Looking forward to it.

Her response is welcome. I haven't overstepped by sharing my safe return to the station. I resist the urge to reply in kind instantly, only for a brief time. I'm petrified to put myself out there but happy it's with her.

Me: Same here.

I push my thoughts away and finish the report for last night's call before the end of my shift.

I drive home and immediately change to swim. By the end of the first lap, I remember Asha's effervescent smile. She lit up every room she entered. Lap two has me believing that my daughter would be a great swimmer by now. Crushing the competition with her mad skills. We didn't settle on a name, but I was partial to Alicia. Asha's gravestone is inscribed with her name and a daughter born sleeping. I linger on my thoughts about my daughter as I travel the length of the pool. My third point I state on my fourth lap today. Every member of my crew made it safely out of the warehouse. A few miles later, I offer my final thought of the day. I'm improving my personal life by going on my second first date tomorrow. Unlike with Piper, I'm not nervous. Perhaps it's the fact Carly was there when I lost my family, and we talked about it. I don't need to parse out when to share my past with Carly. She already knows. My reasoning to solely date a nonlocal may have been flawed. Then again, most townspeople completely avoided me after I lost my family. Retreating into solitude was easy when only my mother and sister were checking in. Not even Asha's family made an effort. At first, their lack of interest in my well-being irked me. I've accepted their absence as a coping mechanism so many years later. Maybe correct, maybe not. Doesn't matter to me.

I finish four thousand yards in the pool, which is about 2.5 miles. I shower and prepare some food. Planning our date is pretty much done in my head. I pad to my office and verify some information before reaching out later.

Just after six, she beats me to it.

"Hi, Carly."

"I hope you don't mind I called you instead."

"Honestly?

I imagine her wrinkling her nose. It's an endearing mannerism Carly does when she's unsure.

"I would prefer the truth, yes."

Here goes nothing. "I've been keeping myself busy so as to not call you too soon."

"You can reach out whenever and however you want."

Once her response registers, a calmness settles over me. Dating is different now. My first attempt was a few years ago, when I jumped into swiping left and right. It was awful, as were the dates I set up. This time I resolved to do it the old-fashioned way, if possible. "Same goes for you. Are you into surprises, or do you need every single scrap of information you can get?"

"I don't mind a secret itinerary, but I have a strong need to be prepared. Does that make sense?"

"Completely. Are you a morning person?"

She giggles. "I attempt to sleep in on the weekends, but I'll make an exception for our date."

"Much appreciated. I would like to be at Acadia by nine." I'm a tad bummed we won't be able to see the peregrine falcons. The nesting area is closed off during mating season. An outdoor date is a wholly new experience for me. I'm excited for tomorrow.

"So, leaving at six?"

"Yes, please."

"No problem. I assume it's colder at the peak?"

I try not to compare her to Asha, who hated the outdoors. "Yes, it will be."

"I'll wear layers."

Good girl. Those two words echo in my mind. I'm thankful I didn't utter them aloud. "Do you need to be back by a certain time?"

"Bedtime?" There is a long pause before she adds, "That sounds weirdly suggestive. I don't have any other plans tomorrow except for our date."

"Perfect. Tell me something new about you?"

"Like?" she asks.

"I'm a huge fan of summer but not the tourists. What is your favorite season?" I shift in my living room chair.

"Winter. The peacefulness of freshly fallen snow, a roaring fire, and a great thriller equal an ideal day for me. Although I might change my mind if I lived upstate where snowfall is heavier."

"Fair enough. What does work-life balance look like for you?"

"Second question of the evening and we're digging in."

"You don't have to answer." I retracted immediately.

"No, it isn't that. Deep is good. I like you aren't sticking to easy things. It doesn't help us decide to move forward together if the inquiries are solely basic likes and dislikes. My job is mostly—I stress mostly—consistent. I work the day shift. I foresee covering some extra time if I can't come to an agreement with my staff though. I try to spend time with my friends at least once a month. What about you?"

"Outside of book club?" I ask.

"I have no idea what you're talking about." She feigns stupidity about the group she heads, which was created by my mother. Before I can answer, she bursts into a fit of laughter. "No need for me to fib with you, is there?"

"Nope."

She sighs. "The book club itself is great. I like reading the same novel as the other members and discussing it. The matchmaking part is…. At first, I liked it. Pairing off deserving friends and coworkers was fun. Our success rate is excellent. Now though, we're receiving pushback and requests to be removed from our list, if you will. We're probably nearing the end."

"I'm sorry."

"Thanks. I mean even Landry asked to be deleted because he claims to be in a relationship. Why would he not introduce me to this woman?"

Damn! I can't tell her who Landry is dating. I mean, sure I could, but those HR forms are confidential. *Are they confidential like HIPPA forms? No, but still.* "I don't know. He will when he's ready."

She scoffs. "Enough about Landry and the probable end of matchmaking in York Beach. What does work-life balance mean to you?"

"Like you, my schedule is usually consistent. The occasional call has our shifts ending later. I'm kind of a homebody, otherwise. I have family meals with my mom and sister usually once a month. Mostly though, I work, swim, and spend time in my shop." Only my sister and mother are aware of that hobby. Divulging it to Carly doesn't make me nervous. It's nice to know I can trust her with the information.

"What do you do?"

"I do woodworking."

"Like furniture?"

"Sometimes. I make all kinds of things like furniture, chess sets, and trinket boxes. Have you been to the Marginal Way recently?"

"No."

The Marginal Way is a walking path along the water in a nearby town. "There are four benches I built along the path."

"That's amazing."

"Thanks. It isn't common knowledge though."

Her response is guarded. "Because?"

I own the stab of grief in my heart. "I started building furniture soon after graduating from college because Asha and I were broke. She had student loans coming out of her ears for her degree. Our goal was to pay them off as quickly as possible. I built what I could to further our plan. I also don't share with anyone."

"Thank for you trusting me with a private piece of your life."

"You're welcome."

"Maybe you can show me your creations someday."

"I would like that." It will be nice to allow someone new to see that portion of me.

We chat for a bit longer. I end the call and consider jumping into the pool again but decide against it. Our conversation was good, and I'm looking forward to learning and sharing more tomorrow. I turn in a little early.

The next morning, after showering and dressing warmly, I prepare coffee for me and tea for Carly. I glance at the clock, grab our supplies, and head to her house.

I'm fully expecting Carly to be sleepy when I arrive. In fact, I find the opposite. She's bright-eyed and sitting on her porch when I arrive.

"Am I late?" I ask as I approach her.

Carly's smile lights up the air around her. *Like Asha.* "Not at all. I'm a little excited."

"Me too." Resisting the urge to hold her again is impossible. I slide my arm around Carly's waist and hug her against me briefly. She relaxes against me, and I catalog the softness of her curves. I thought my physical attraction to her was an anomaly. More importantly, I expected the sexual tension between us to fizzle out. I was wrong. I release her slowly to inhale the sweetness of her perfume longer. This scent is lighter than the one the other day. "Ready?"

"Let's go."

I grab her backpack from the porch and offer her my arm. Once she settles into the passenger seat, I stow her backpack and round the car.

"Do you have a caffeine addiction?" she asks, noticing the two travel mugs in the cup holders.

"No. One of those is for you."

"Thank you. I don't drink coffee though."

I grin at her. I lift one cup and extend it to her. "This is tea with some milk and sugar." Before she can respond, I back out of her driveway.

Carly is stunned silent for a moment. Then she asks, "How did you know?"

"There's no coffee maker in your kitchen and a kettle on the stove."

She takes a sip from her cup. "This is perfect. What else did you observe about me?"

"You're highly organized. The frames in your living room indicate you love your brother and friends. I didn't see any images of your parents, which makes sense given what you shared about them. I would be willing to bet you prefer books over movies over television."

"Wow! Those statements are eerily on point. Any of those apply to you?"

"The orderly part. I have photos but less than you. Your order of preference for entertainment is correct. I don't really choose to relax in that way." I pull onto the interstate and head north toward Acadia National Park.

"What are you building now?"

I pause for a fraction too long.

"You don't —"

Shaking my head, "I want to. I have a commission at the moment. I'm trying to recall if there's a privacy request attached."

"Either way, it's fine. What trail are we hiking?"

"There are a bunch of options. How far are you thinking?"

Carly shrugs. "Four or five easy miles is good. Three strenuous ones is doable as well."

"The Ocean Path is 4.4 miles and has ocean views."

Carly chuckles softly. Her laugh is music to my soul.

"Then there's Jordan Pond or Acadia Mountain. Both are three miles or less but more difficult."

"Any of those will work for me."

I don't dig into her agreeableness right now. We're getting to know each other. The rest of the ride passes smoothly. We discuss the game a little bit as well as the upcoming First In, Last Out Ball. "Are you spearheading that event as well?"

"No, I declined. I believe the Women's Auxiliary at York Memorial is handling it. I'm glad they took over. I don't have time with my staff threatening to unionize."

"Not going well?" I ask and pull off the exit ramp into the park. After paying the entrance fee, I choose a spot at the trailhead near Beehive Lagoon.

"I'm not sure. The demands aren't awful… understandable even, but I truly don't have space in the budget despite Scott leaving."

We grab our gear and walk to the trail. Side by side, we traverse the trail unless another group needs to pass us. The ocean crashing against the rock formations and gorgeous foliage doesn't compare to Carly. Sure, it's beautiful, but she's fun and vibrant. Her sunny disposition is surprising given the floor she commands at the hospital. The gore and heartbreak of the emergency room doesn't crush her. On top of her demeanor, she's beautiful. Her curves would make any man beg. Never mind me who hasn't been with anyone in years.

My mind is wandering about her physical beauty so much that I miss her calling me from the fenced jut out near the water.

"Coming."

"This is stunning. Can we take a photo?"

"Sure." I extend her phone out to snap a selfie.

A younger couple approaches. "Would you like me to take that for you?" I brunette offers.

"Yes, thank you," Carly answers, and I hand her the phone.

I draw Carly close and look down at her. The urge to kiss her washes over me like the tide rolling toward the shore. I refrain though from fear and not wanting to have an audience. My wife was the last woman I kissed how I want to kiss Carly. Perhaps I'm not as ready for dating as I thought I was. I push that worry away instantly. If my mother can move forward, so can I. I purposely don't go down the intimacy road with my mom and Mr. Kingman in mind.

The young woman takes a few photos and returns Carly's phone. "You two are gorgeous together. Have a nice hike."

"Thank you. You as well," I manage to reply.

We turn and watch the waves and the scenery for a few minutes. I find myself staring at her instead of the view.

She gifts me with a huge smile when she catches me. Without hesitation, she curls her arms around me and sets her head on my chest. I exhale slowly and rest my chin atop her head.

"You good?" she asks, glancing up at me with slight concern etched on her flawless face.

"Yeah, why?"

"Your heart is racing."

I pull my lips into a tight line. My body is betraying me.

"Do I make you nervous?" she mumbles against my chest.

More than you know. Be honest. Own it. "Yes."

She doesn't press but waits me out.

"I like you…" *A lot, a whole lot.* "… and it scares the hell out of me."

Carly inhales sharply and meets my gaze. "Me too. I won't hurt you purposely."

"Same."

"Slow and steady work for you?" she asks.

"Yes."

I kiss the top of her head, and we meander along the rest of the trail, chatting and having a wonderful time.

Our ride home is quieter but not uncomfortably so. On the way to her house, I stop for pizza in the village.

We curl up on her patio, eat, and chat for hours about distant memories like how I met Asha, and current happenings, including the upcoming game and my promotion.

The most important part of our conversation is setting up time to see her again on Thursday.

Near seven, I leave for the evening after a long hug and a kiss on her cheek. As far as first dates go, ours was wonderful. We met all our requirements and planned a second one.

CHAPTER TEN

CARLY

Tossing and turning is no fun. However, at least the reason I can't sleep is good. Given the example of love and marriage my parents provided me, I'm skeptical that one man could be perfect for me. Yet, all day long... Alden was honest and vocal about his feelings and fears. I'm grateful, especially since I'm terrified as well. My reasons for keeping distance between us in a romantic way was mainly based on my presence in the emergency room when he lost his family. He has no clue I was interested in him in high school but never shared. Not sure I would divulge those feelings now either.

With a massive cup of tea in hand and a second one in a travel mug, I hustle to work, hoping to make it in on time.

"Pushing it a little," Willa accuses as I hurry past her in the lobby.

"I know. Didn't sleep well."

"Why?" she asks.

I turn and shake my head. I don't want her to get the impression he spent the night or anything. Then again, Willa and Scarlett would probably cheer me on mightily if Alden and I did twist up my sheets yesterday. "Will talk with you more later."

The idea of being with him doesn't scare me except for the baggage we bring into this. Steady progress both in learning about each other and the intimacy works for me, despite my urge to feel his rippled abs beneath my fingertips and if his lips are truly as soft as they felt against my cheek.

I clock in and chuck my stuff into my office. I'm paged over the intercom when I'm halfway to the emergency room. As I listen to the details, I pick up my pace and find chaos. There was a multicar accident near the high school, including buses, cars, and pedestrians. My floor is flooded with patients and concerned parents. The injured were transported by overfilled ambulances, parents, and even some classmates who weren't involved in the accident. The passengers of a small sedan at the front of the school and the children in the first bus bore the brunt of the injuries. All told, five buses and two cars were involved. Luckily, the buses were mostly empty.

I grab Janie and Mik and request they follow me to the waiting room.

"Ladies and gentlemen, if I could have your attention." The rumble of chatter doesn't decrease. Clamoring and shouting for updates continue around me.

My height is not helping me today. I climb onto a chair and use Mikel's shoulder as a balance point. "Excuse me, if you could direct your focus over here." I repeat the sentence three times before the roar dies down enough for me to provide guidance.

"I understand you're seeking information about your children. Please organize in bus number order from left to right in the rear of this room. If your child is a pedestrian or in a personal vehicle, please form a line against the window. We will provide more details as soon as we can."

The crowd moves into the areas as I requested.

"Mik, please start at one end and gather as much information as possible. Janie, take the other side. I'm going to have the staff get the name and bus number information. Once I have an update, we'll escort the parents either back to see their child or to the cafeteria where we can reunite them."

"Questions?"

Both shake their heads and get to work. I return to the nurse's station and share my plan with the staff. I assist in checking on the lesser injured patients to expedite moving them out of the treatment areas and the hallway. I'm calm cool and collected. I thrive bringing order to chaos.

Two hours into my day, I'm returning to the floor after reuniting thirty kids with their parents. The extent of their injuries range from a small laceration or needing a once-over to confirm a lack of serious concerns. I held up two students for further observation with potential concussions.

Upon my return, the influx of people has diminished from the high school accident. I make my rounds and check in with my staff. The adult driver of the sedan is in CT, and his daughter is being treated for a large laceration on her forehead. She was exiting the car when the bus collided with the rear end. She was jostled and hit her head on the doorframe. Our plastic surgeon is excellent. She should have minimal, if any, scarring. Unfortunately, it won't be completely healed before prom.

One more trip to the cafeteria and I have decreased the patient and parent count to manageable numbers, and the waiting room is nearly empty. The downside is the mountains of charting and paperwork that needs to be completed from a large event such as this one.

Early in the afternoon, I trudge to my office to eat some of my prepared lunch. When I arrive, I find a bag hanging on my doorknob.

I lift it and enter my office. Only then do I look at my phone. I have a bunch of text messages. The first one is from my brother.

Landry: Please accept lunch as a peace offering. I should've told you about Alden, and my girlfriend. Let me know when we can have dinner… the three of us.

I'm not sure if he means us plus his girlfriend or us and Alden. Am I ready for that? Sharing about our date, sure but a meal? *Hypocrite.* Not really. We're comparing one date to six months. Plus, Alden is Landry's boss.

Me: Thank you. I look forward to dinner.

Before checking out the rest of my messages, I tear into the white paper and take a huge bite of the sandwich. The deliciousness hits my soul.

Alden: I hope you have come up for air from the accident at York High.

Alden: Will you let me cook dinner for you tonight?

My heart swoons. If anyone can understand the stress and strain of a multiple casualty event, it's him.

Me: Just sat down with my lunch. I would love to have dinner with you.

Alden: 6 at my place? Any allergies or no-go foods?

Me: No allergies. I'll try any food once. What is your address?

Alden: Great. See you later. 42 Linden Place.

I'm not going to overthink this. The man I'm dating offered to prepare dinner for me after a particularly busy shift. Nor am I going to worry about seeing him two days in a row despite agreeing to a slower pace.

I spend the afternoon in the corner of the nurses' station, updating charts and inputting information to assist my team. All but the driver of the sedan have been discharged. He is being held for observation.

I wrap up and gather my things from my office. Unfortunately, I don't find a clean hoodie or nicer shirt to wear to dinner. I shrug and head out the rear exit to the parking garage.

When I step off the elevator at the garage, Janie is walking to her car as well.

"Thank you for your help today. It isn't your job."

Inwardly, I frown and reply, "You're welcome. My role is to keep the ER running smoothly. I'll do whatever is necessary to make that happen."

She nods and adds, "We appreciated it immensely. Good night."

As Janie leaves, it dawns on me that my staff knows my salary and benefits are separate from their contract. These negotiations won't impact me, at least not monetarily or with extra time off. Chances are, my hours are going to increase.

I shake off the conversation and drive to Alden's. His home is located on the outskirts of town. The large colonial sits at the end of a long winding driveway. It's quiet and peaceful. When I get out of my car, Alden is waiting for me on the front porch.

"How was your afternoon?" he asks after hauling me into his arms.

He's warm. I didn't realize I was cold until he held me close. "Not bad. There were only two serious injuries. Once I got the crowd organized, it was mostly paperwork. You?"

He tilts his head toward the door. "Let's get you inside." Alden links our hands and leads me into his home. Once inside, he disappears through a door to the right.

It's clear that he lives here alone. Gladys and Essie haven't commented about his décor or attempted to make it softer either. It's bare and clinical-looking. The kitchen is gorgeous with granite countertops and stainless appliances, including a sizable island with prep sink.

When he returns, he hands me a YFD hoodie. "If you need it. You shivered when I held you."

"Thanks." I am cold, but the shiver was from him not the chill in the air this evening. Probably not the right time to mention that little tidbit though. Slipping my arm into the sleeve, I pull it overhead. It's huge on me and super soft. I roll the cuffs to make the sleeves manageable. I kind of love feeling wrapped in an Alden-scented cocoon, although the real one is miles better. "Can I give you a hand?"

He smiles at me, and I swear my heart flutters. "I was off today. Please let me take care of you. The food is done. I just need to plate it."

Silently, I wait and follow him to the dining table. It's heavy and looks like oak, but that's a guess. Wood species are not my thing. It's oval-shaped with six chairs. Each one has a rounded top to mimic the curve of the table. He sets down our plates and pulls out my chair.

I sigh softly, thank him, then ask, "Did you build this?"

A proud smile graces his chiseled face. One where the sexy dimple is prominent. "Yeah, I did."

"It's beautiful."

He acknowledges the compliment, then adds, "That is chicken stir-fry with broccoli, peppers, cashews, and onions over white rice."

"Looks delish." I savor the first bite. Then eat a few more before sharing my review. "I give it five stars."

He laughs and visibly relaxes.

"What else did you do today aside from pull off a culinary delight?"

Alden shakes his head. "Normal stuff. I worked out, had a late breakfast with my sister, and then delivered my latest project."

"As well as monitoring the public safety calls." I raise an eyebrow as if he has another choice.

"Yes, but only to know if I needed to go into work. You don't?"

I drop my head in silent acquiescence. "While I rarely take a scheduled day off, I listen too—"

"Just in case." Alden finishes my thought.

First responders are cut from the same cloth. We have an inherent need to serve our community in our chosen capacity. For me, it's nursing the sick and injured while Alden protects people and property.

I grin and finish my meal. We clear the table and move into the kitchen. Side by side, we clean our dishes.

"Want to sit outside or inside?" he asks.

"Outside."

With our hands threaded together, Alden leads me through the French doors into the backyard. It's stunning. As expected, there's an indoor in-ground pool. I can see it through the massive windows. The sitting area has a couch and two chairs along with a propane firepit.

I glance up and note the sky above us. It isn't quite dark yet, but I bet the canopy of stars will be magnificent.

"What are you thinking?" he asks.

"It's soothing back here."

"It is." He guides me to the couch and lights the fire.

Soon a decent wave of heat wafts in our direction. Alden sits in the corner and draws me into his embrace. My head is tucked beneath his chin as if it's a perfect fit. If I'm being honest with myself, I like being here with him. Part of me always wondered if we would be a good match. So far, we are.

"Do you sit out here often?" I ask.

"Not really."

Why didn't he tell me? "Oh, we could go inside," I offer.

He shakes his head over mine. "No, this is…."

I pull back slightly and look up at him. His chocolate eyes are teeming with emotion. There's a brawl happening in his mind, but I have no idea the topic.

I shift and add a bit of space between us. "Want to share your thoughts?"

He takes a few deep breaths.

"When you're ready, I'll listen."

Alden answers, "I do. I'm not sure how."

"Brutal honesty. It's the only way given our intertwined background." I have no doubt his wife and daughter are in his thoughts daily. I don't blame him. Most would believe our professions desensitize us to death. It's quite the opposite in my experience. We can compartmentalize while working but also understand the need to handle our feelings somehow. After particularly difficult days, some of my coworkers drink heavily while some meditate. Others exercise to the point of exhaustion. If I had to guess, that is Alden's coping mechanism.

He shifts on the cushion so we're fully facing each other. One of our legs is between us while the other is over the side, dangling toward the floor. Alden's hands are balled into tight fists in his lap. Without a second thought, I take one and slowly open it, then repeat with the other hand.

"Brutal?" he asks.

I steel myself for what he may say but reply, "Yes."

"I have been mentally comparing you to Asha."

Well, damn! Not what I was expecting him to say.

"All of this is foreign to me. I have been on exactly four dates since my wife died. Two were years ago, one with Piper—if you could even call it that—and hiking with you. I suppose dinner tonight is a date as well so five." He pauses as if he's never shared that or what he's about to say with anyone before. "I knew what I was looking for… and yet, you…. For example, Asha hated the outdoors, and you willingly went on a hike and opted to sit under the stars. I'm fighting with what I thought I wanted and who you are."

The turbulence in his gaze has lessened, but it's still present. I wait him out.

He continues, "When we were in Acadia after the woman snapped our picture, my mind was in a similar place."

"But?"

"Not a but exactly." He lifts one of his hands and drags his thumb along my lower lip.

It takes restraint not to sigh or lick my lips.

"I wanted to kiss you. Still do." Alden's eyelids clamp down tightly, and he adds, "I feel like I'm betraying Asha with every happy moment I spend with you and each time I consider the less than honorable things I desire to do to you." He opens his eyes and meets mine.

I raise an eyebrow. *Yes, please.* "As selfish as this is going to sound, you met your obligation to Asha. I'm confident you and I wouldn't be having this conversation if she were alive."

He frowns briefly after processing my statement. "Would you have gone out with me sooner?"

I purse my lips while parsing out whether to divulge my long-standing pining. *Absolutely.* "Yes, but our conversation about my presence after the accident would've still happened. Perhaps it was a secret because you were with Asha, but even in high school, if you asked, I would've agreed."

Alden's gaze lifts skyward. "I didn't know."

No reason for me not to share. "It took me a while to reconcile being on Asha's care team and failing to help her and your baby. By that point, you were...."

"Reclusive?" he suggests.

I nod tightly, unable to say the word myself, and keep my line of sight on our joined hands.

"Carly." His voice trembling with emotion.

I look up at him. The storminess captured on his face has mostly dissipated. I'm not sure who leans in first. Perhaps it was a joint effort, but the initial touch of his lips to mine is tentative and sweet. Sparks zip from my mouth to my toes and directly to my head. If he feels the same flutter in his chest, I expect him to draw back.

He doesn't.

Instead, he drags his tongue along my lower lip before dipping into my mouth. Containing a whimper from the undercurrent of sensations flowing through me is difficult, but I pull it off. Barely. The tenor moves from friendly and tentative to passionate heat in milliseconds. His hands slide to my face, and our lips fuse together.

Alden's lips are as soft as I imagined, maybe even more so. His kiss is the perfect blend of pressure and teasing. My fingernails slide down his chest before slipping beneath the hem of his shirt. The heat from only my fingertips on his finely honed abs is intense. Never has a first kiss felt like this. He travels over to my ear, then down the slope of my neck.

Containing soft murmurs is impossible. It's been quite some time since I was kissed properly, and I want more. So much more. With that thought looming in my mind, I add a sliver of space between us.

"As much as I would like to continue this, I need to go home. I have to work tomorrow." Each word is true. Also true is the fact that if I don't leave now, our choices may be questionable for a second date at this point. For us to maintain slow and steady at least.

Alden acknowledges my words and skims his lips across mine. He pushes to standing and offers me his hand.

I take it but don't rise to my feet.

"What's wrong, beautiful?"

"Nothing." My answer is unintentionally sharp. No man has ever made me feel that much from a kiss, let alone the first one.

He tilts his head in question and adds, "Car—"

"It's never felt like that before." My voice is so soft and low I'm sure he can't hear me.

To my surprise, he replies, "For me either."

My chest tightens with the ramifications of his words, but I don't address them aloud. "Thank you for knowing I needed to decompress after work."

"You're welcome. When are you free next?"

I laugh. "Thursday dinner and then we're meeting for the game planning with Lachlan and Lacey after your next shift."

"We are. Can we go out the next day?"

"Yes."

He smiles widely, grabs my hand, and leads me through the house. At the front door, I start to remove his hoodie.

"Keep it. It looks much better on you."

I wrinkle my nose, rise onto my toes, and kiss him good night.

"Please text me when you get home?" he asks.

"I will."

After I grab my purse, Alden escorts me to my car. I'm not worried about anyone seeing us, not here, but are we keeping our budding relationship quiet for now?

I pull away with that thought swimming in my mind. Willa and Scarlett already know. For now, I plan to keep our exceptional first kiss between us and drive home.

After opening my front door, I send him a text and call it a night.

Me: I'm home. Talk to you soon.

Alden: Sweet dreams, beautiful.

Me: Same to you.

Alden: Me? Beautiful?

Me: Absolutely. You might be carved from marble.

Alden: As are you. I'm blushing over here.

Me: xoxo

Alden: xoxo

With our texting complete for now, I turn in and realize that even though work was crappy, Alden knew and helped me deal with it. I'm grateful beyond measure.

CHAPTER ELEVEN

ALDEN

I've completed my next uneventful shift, and upon returning home, I dive into the pool. My thoughts follow the regular pattern.

Asha knew my moods. When to push and when to give me space. It seems Carly does too. She *read* me like an open book. The blonde with curves that don't quit saw me struggling with my emotions and gave me the choice and space to share.

Alicia would be active in her school community, like the student council.

As I swim, I ponder a positive aspect of my day. Carly. I didn't feel guilty thinking about her, reliving our first kiss over and over. I need to remind myself repeatedly that finding a woman to spend my time with isn't a betrayal of my marriage vows. I reach to twist the band on my ring finger. It isn't there. It never was. I never had to force myself to take it off after she died either. Rafael believes that was a double-edged sword for me. Asha and I were struggling early on, and we sold everything we could to dig out of our debt, including all our jewelry like Asha's engagement ring and diamond studs to our wedding rings. We felt an outward sign wasn't necessary if we were fully committed to each other. Sadly, we were still working on the loans when she died.

The water flows over me, and I decide on my next action item: ask Carly to the ball. You would think my chest might seize and I would be worried she might decline. She won't, not after that kiss or purposely scheduling time to see each other.

I hop out of the pool and grab a protein shake. Before showering, I order flowers. I'll pick them up on my way to her place for our meeting. We're supposed to be there at seven. I plan to be early so I can give her the flowers and perhaps ask her to the ball.

I reconsider what to do with my time until I need to leave and walk out to my shop. I don't have any commissions at the moment. Carly's appreciation for the dining table was palpable and genuine. Ideas and plans crash though my mind about something I could build for her. Then the perfect gift hits me. I pull out my sketch pad and draw. A few hours later, I have a full-fledged plan and a list of lumber and other materials. The next step will be ordering the supplies and getting to work.

First, I need to clean up and get over to Carly's before Hagen and Lacey. Later than I wanted but still earlier than expected, I arrive at her home.

I knock and hear, "Coming."

When she answers the door, a huge smile grows on her face. She's fresh out of the shower and not wearing any makeup. Her skin is flawless. Without a second thought, she rises on her toes and kisses me.

The same heat from the last time I saw her returns. Sliding my arm around her waist, I then lift her and elbow the front door closed. Her legs wrap effortlessly around me. I take a few long strides and set her on the granite island. I drop the flowers behind her, cup her face, and greet her properly. The warmth surrounding my memories of our first kiss weren't overblown.

Our tongues tangle, and her fingernails bite into my shoulder blades. Each second takes a little more of my breath away. By the time we break apart, we're both panting.

"Hi," I manage after staring at her waiting for my heart rate to decrease. It does but not much. "How was your day at work?"

"Good except for the negotiations. I foresee a huge problem. The board isn't budging."

"I'm sorry."

She shrugs. "Me too. What about you?"

"Normal day-off stuff. Errands, workout, and spending time with you."

Carly wrinkles her nose then pushes out her lower lip.

I want to tug that lip between my teeth and kiss her more.

"We won't be alone," she reminds me.

"Not ideal but… we will be for our date."

She smiles at the reminder then adds, "Are we going to be able to pull this off?"

"What?" I ask while tucking a strand of hair behind her ear.

"Discretion with Hagen and Lacey."

"I don't mind if people know we're dating, but I would like to navigate it privately for a bit longer. Do you?"

She pauses a little too long for my liking. "I'm a private person as well. Our relationship is our business. No one else's."

"I agree. Now that I've held you and kissed you, keeping my distance won't be easy."

"Same here."

Rather than talk more about disclosing our relationship widely, we kiss until her doorbell rings. We laugh softly.

"Stash these flowers for now, and I'll get the door," Alden states

"Okay."

I bracket her hips and set her on the hardwood floor. I settle myself before greeting her guest.

If I didn't know Hagen personally, his imposing stature would make me pause. "Hey, Hagen. Come in." I close the door behind him.

We bro hug. "Good to see you, Rhodes. I thought Landry was working with his sister on this for the YFD."

"He was but asked me to step in."

"Cool."

"How are your girls?" Hagen is a K-9 officer with the YPD. He was a single dad to Lilah until the matchmakers fixed him up with Eva Washington. They have been married for a year and are expecting a son any day.

"Great. How are Gladys and Essie?"

"Doing well."

There's a soft knock on the door. I answer it and greet Lacey. "Hey." Lacey is an EMT. She's petite with girl-next-door vibes and a huge mastiff named Barkley.

"I was expecting someone prettier than you to answer the door," she quips.

"Carly was busy." I check the thoughts in my head. Without a doubt, my face is beet red recalling her touch and how she fits in my hands.

"No problem. Just weird for you to answer the door at someone else's house."

Not if you're dating. The idea of a relationship with Carly doesn't scare me at all. It's progress and I'll accept it willingly.

We congregate near the island then move into the dining room with drinks, and Carly joins us.

"Thank you for coming. I hope to keep this short and sweet so you can get back to your weekend plans."

Hagen speaks first. "I have the youth league handling the entrance and security patrols at the rec plex. As of this afternoon, six teams are drafted and ready to participate. I'll have roster sheets and jerseys ready to hand off at the registration table. I expect them to be delivered next week. Eva and I will sort them by team then."

"Great. Thank you. Lacey?" Carly turns her attention to the next item on her list.

I have been staring at Carly since she started running this meeting. She's mesmerizing when she's in charge. Hell, her snuggled against me under a blanket of stars is otherworldly as well. I redirect my gaze to the list on the table.

"The medical tent is set. Penn agreed to run it rather than play. Basic first aid kits will be in each dugout."

She's quite the taskmaster. Carly checks off the next two items on her list and then asks me. "What about the volunteers?"

"I spoke with Gugliotti and Craven. They will provide upper classmen to earn community service credit. Do you have a minimum number in mind?"

She taps her pointer finger on the sheet in front of her. "Maybe ten if they plan to stay all day. Twenty if they are doing it in shifts like the flag football game."

I acknowledge her. "I'll let them know."

"Thanks."

I didn't realize it until I look over at Hagen and Lacey. They are silent, observing my exchange with Carly. Apparently, I wasn't as discreet in my admiration earlier or my feelings are plastered on my face. Both statements could be, and probably are, accurate.

Blunt as ever, Lacey asks, "How long have you two been dating? The heat in this room is off the charts. It has nothing to do with me or Lachlan."

"What she said," Hagen adds, pointing toward Lacey.

Carly blushes instantly. She glances in my direction and replies without looking back at Lacey, "It's new, and we would appreciate discretion."

Well done. I couldn't have said it better myself.

Lacey answers quickly. "No problem. I would be remiss if I didn't add you make a gorgeous couple."

"We appreciate that," I reply. She isn't wrong, although I would say the beauty is all Carly.

Within the next thirty minutes, Carly finishes her checklist, and our event planning assistants leave. Overall, we're mostly set for the game in six weeks.

I clear the table of our glasses while Carly shows them out. She joins me in the kitchen and links her hands around my waist.

"Good job handling her question. I would've stumbled with what to say."

"You agree?"

I tilt my head. "Yes. I don't want to keep us a secret for long, but I would like a little longer before the entire town is in our business. Both of us are private. I'm sure Willa and Scarlett are aware of our dates, right?"

Carly nods in agreement. "I needed to tell someone. Plus, they knew about before."

Confused, I ask, "I'm sorry, what?"

"They are my besties. They know I would've agreed to a date a long time ago."

"What other details did you share with them?"

"We have clear boundaries about how much we divulge."

"Meaning?" I ask in keen interest.

Carly pulls her lower lip between her teeth before replying, "We don't discuss anything past we kissed or we had sex. I didn't share that our first kiss was the best I've ever had. Nor did I tell my girls that it was difficult to leave. What about you? Did you tell Essie anything?"

I laugh. "No. Essie isn't my sounding board for relationship advice. She's great for other things. If my sister had her way, I would be remarried and have a gaggle of kids. Chemistry and compatibility be damned."

"Oh."

"I understand her position. She's younger and blissfully happy with Halston. She just wants the same for me." W*e are heading in the right direction.* "I have a friend I met in my grief group named Rafael. He lost his partner a few months before Asha's death. He has been pushing me for years. He recently got remarried himself."

"Good. We all need someone to talk to."

"What shall we do now that we're alone?" I ask.

"Do you have time for a movie?"

"I don't have anywhere to go. Plus, I'm off tomorrow, and I have a hot date. Not sure where we're going, but she assured me it would be fun."

"Anyone I know?" she jokes.

I draw her into my arms. It's weird to admit, but she fits. An even more daunting thought is I miss her when we're apart. "You know her well in fact."

"Me?"

"Yeah, you." I laugh and lower my lips to hers. Each touch of her mouth on mine ripples through my entire body. I was honest when I indicated it wasn't like this with Asha. Fear slices through me despite the overwhelmingly pleasant reactions to Carly's skin beneath my fingers. My experience with women is limited and another layer of worry for my fledgling relationship. Pulling back slightly, I ask, "What movie are you thinking?"

She shrugs and leads me to the couch. We settle in the corner, and Carly snuggles against me. Thankfully, Carly is none the wiser to my thoughts this time. She hands over the remotes. I navigate to *The Union,* featuring Halle Berry and Mark Wahlberg.

It's a fun movie. I watch most of it. Near the end though, I catch myself cataloguing the dusting of freckles on her nose. I didn't realize it until I met her. I want her close to me physically. Even a small touch point calms me.

After the film finishes, Carly escorts me to the door. Honestly, the last thing I want to do is leave.

"When will you be ready in the morning?"

She smiles. "Not knowing is killing you, huh?"

I hold my thumb and index finger close together. "A little bit."

"Eight, please."

I nod.

"Good night, Alden." Carly slides her arms around me and flattens them on my back. Her head rests on my chest.

I hold her closer. I kiss the top of her head and add, "Sweet dreams, Carly."

It's difficult to urge my feet to move out the door. She's a force to be reckoned with. Damn if I don't want every minute possible to find out how to do exactly that.

CHAPTER TWELVE

CARLY

Waking before my alarm on a weekend is a new experience for me. Then again, I'm not normally excited for plans like I am today. Not completely true. Spending time with Alden is a more accurate reason. The sun is peeking through my curtains. Content to start my day, I shut off my alarm and pad to the bathroom.

Once showered and dressed, I make tea and scroll through my phone. Unfortunately, I learn the deadline for an agreement has passed. The only solace I can take is the staff agreed to continue negotiating rather than strike. The accommodation is only for thirty more days. My honest approach with the board and my staff seems to have garnered dividends. I was forthright with both sides. The board felt the staff would blink, and denied access to the rainy-day fund. My nurses and support team decreased their hourly demand in both monetary amount and length but refused to budge on the additional personal time off. Hopefully, the board will move a little, and we can figure out a new contract before they unionize. I highly doubt another extension is in my future. More importantly, I refuse to let that bad news ruin my day with Alden.

Alden arrives a few minutes early. "Good morning, gorgeous," he greets me when I answer the door.

He's hot! Alden chose chino shorts and a graphic tee that stretches across his impressive chest. "Hi. You look pretty good yourself."

"I guessed on the attire since my date refused to share our destination."

I feign innocence. "Who, me?" I kiss him lightly, slip my arm into my tote, and follow him outside.

"Yes, you." After opening my door and rounding the car, he asks, "Where to?"

"We're going to the game at Fenway. Before that, we can check out either Faneuil Hall or the aquarium. Your choice."

I could get used to this. Him. Us. I want to. Before I can add more, his mouth is on mine, and he's kissing me deeply. A few sultry minutes later, he pulls back and asks, "Did I tell you I love baseball?"

"No."

He continues, "Did I mention I've always wanted to go to a game at the Green Monster?"

"No. What I'm hearing is I planned the best date ever?" Warmth spreads through me. Perhaps despite my previous failures and lack of a good example, I can date well.

Glee is plastered on his chiseled face. "Yeah, you did." He presses a quick kiss to my lips and pulls onto the road.

The ride is slightly more than an hour. We park in a garage near Boston Common. I picked this city for the game, but it does help that we won't run into anyone from York Beach today. At least we shouldn't anyway.

With our hands threaded together we walk around the area and take in the beautiful gardens. Boston Common, America's oldest botanical garden, is marked with views along the water as well as fragrant flowers and colorful trees, including cherry blossoms. The light pink hue is fantastic.

"What else are you willing to share about yourself?" I ask as we wander down the pathway.

"What would you like to learn?"

"Everything."

His gaze meets mine briefly, but he doesn't add more. Something is on his mind. Eventually, he'll tell me.

I press on. "Why Fenway and not Yankee Stadium or Wrigley Field?"

"Are you a closet Yankees fan?" The disdain in his voice is unmistakable.

A laugh bubbles up from deep in my belly. "No. I'm a fan of the game overall. Are you?"

He stops walking, looks left and then right. "Promise you won't share with anyone?"

I pretend to zip my lips.

"I root for the Cubs."

I gasp. "Why?"

Alden shakes his head. "It's one of the oldest teams in the league, and it was my dad's favorite.'"

"I'll allow it."

"Much appreciated."

As we meander through the park, we stop and take a photo with the *Make Way for Ducklings* statues. They're super cute. So far today hasn't been anything over-the-top. It isn't who I am anyway, but... spending time with Alden away from York Beach has been effortless and wonderful. Part of me is surprised, while the small inkling in the recesses of my heart knew all those years ago. The reality is the timing wasn't right then. Now is a different story. We both have personal hangups we need to deal with, but they're out in the open. Mostly.

"Ready to head to Fenway?" I ask.

A huge grin grows on his face. "Isn't it a little early?"

I purse my lips and look up at him. "Not if you're having a stadium tour first."

"Seriously?"

"Yes."

He wraps his arms around my waist and spins us in a circle. Containing my gleeful laugh is impossible. Alden kisses me, then sets me on my feet. "Let's go."

With our hands linked, we hurry back to the car for no reason other than Alden's excitement.

After the car ride, we park and enter the stadium for the tour. Our guide is amazing and points out the history and fun parts of the venue. For example, the seats atop the Green Monster debuted in 2003.

Pure joy is plastered on Alden's face as we listen and learn about the history. The same emotion wells in my chest that I planned this date and was spot-on in my choice. We snap a few pictures along the way, including one near the plaques featuring Babe Ruth and Roger Clemens.

With concession stand snacks in hand, we take our seats. The breeze is crisp and light. The sun is shining down. It's an ideal day to watch a game.

"Behind home plate?" Alden asks.

"Of course. They're the best seats in the house. Comfy chairs and a great view of the field." Today's game is between the Red Sox and the Atlanta Braves. If I knew he rooted for the Cubs, I would've opted to travel to Yankee stadium instead. They have a series with them later in the summer. Maybe we can plan a quick getaway. "You okay?"

"Definitely." His answer is a bit too quick for my liking. Alden is quiet, thoughtful, and precise. He appears calm, cool, and collected. I'm sure it's helpful for his job, but personally his demeanor feels a bit like he's hiding. Shielding himself and me from his feelings isn't a good thing, at least not long term.

The pitch is thrown and immediately fouled off down the first base line. Through six innings, no one has been on base for either team. Our chatter has been limited to strategy and gameplay until now.

"Do you want to go home?" I don't want to end our date, but despite his exuberance before, he hasn't said much. Worry wraps around my heart. Could he be having second thoughts?

"No, not at all."

I tilt my head. "Are you sure? I can see the anguish turning in your mind."

"I'm not upset." He exhales and turns in his seat to face me more fully. "My thoughts are a jumbled mess. Mainly, I'm not used to being taken care of. It's my job."

He didn't say it out loud, but I heard "as the man in my family." I understand why he feels that way, but he deserves to be happy as well.

He continues, "I worry about my mom and Essie as well as my crew and...." Alden drags his hand down his face before gripping his chin. "You. Despite those women being absolutely capable of caring for themselves. A fact my mother and sister point out eloquently and exuberantly when I push too much. Essie also reminds me she has a husband. I suppose now my mother has a boyfriend."

"Why does it bother you that the women in your life care about your well-being?" The answer hits me, but I don't voice it aloud. The last person who doted on him was his wife. Gladys surely didn't go back to mothering him after Asha's death. He's been completely on his own. Then after Mr. Rhodes died, he increased check-ins and the like for his mother and sister. We start dating, and now I'm....

"Bother isn't the right word."

The crack of the bat draws our attention to the field. The home team took the lead with a solo home run.

He continues returning his gaze to me. "I'm... not used to it. I have been a bachelor for... a long time. Until you, my attempts to find a partner haven't gotten further than a cup of coffee. I'm on a roller coaster. On one hand, I'm crazy happy that we're dating. Then I have a rush of pain or grief, or I don't even know what to call it because…."

I thread our fingers, and he takes a deep breath. The remainder of his thought was barely above a whisper, but I heard every miniscule implication.

"… I don't know you well yet, except I'm drawn to you, and our connection even this early is stronger than mine was to Asha. That terrifies me. I loved her and was prepared to build a life with her. Imagining what we could have might be better shakes me to my core."

Oh, Alden. I lean forward and kiss him lightly. "What can I do?"

His eyes meet mine, and the anguish has lessened quite a bit. Alden may keep his thoughts close, but when he shares them, he's relieved. This sexy-as-hell man has a heart of gold. I would be so lucky to hold onto it for the rest of my days.

"Be you, with a little dash of patience to allow me to grapple with our potential," he replies.

"I will."

When I look at the scoreboard, it appears after the home run, the last innings were three up then three down. It's the bottom of the eighth, and the score is unchanged.

When the game ends with no more action, I don't immediately move from my seat while my date stands.

Alden frowns. "Not in a rush?" he asks and sits down.

"I would rather stay here than push my way through the crowd to wait in parking lot. It goes back to my playing days, I guess. The field was always peaceful right before and immediately after a game."

"I understand. I was at the pool at least an hour before every other competitor. After the meet ended, I would wait for the natatorium to empty and deconstruct my win or loss alone. My mom was grateful when I could drive myself."

I stifle the fact that my parents were never present at my softball games despite the ability to do so. My mother was usually unemployed. She had the time but didn't bother. I will be better for my children should I be lucky enough to have some.

Once the crowd thins out, we exit the stadium and walk through the nearly empty parking lot. My tactic works, and we're pulling into my driveway over an hour later.

"Want to come in?" I ask as we reach my front door.

"I should go. I'm on shift in the morning. Today was the best date I've ever been on."

"Our first one was nice as well," I counter.

He purses his lips, and I refraining from cutting off his response just to kiss him. "Allow me to qualify my statement."

"Please do." I wink at him.

"This has been the best date I've ever been on that I didn't plan."

I giggle and step close to him. My need to touch him far exceeds anyone I've ever been with before. "I approve of your new statement."

Alden slides his hands along my jaw to cup my face. "Can I cook for you on Wednesday?"

"Sure. I'll come to your place after work."

Without another word, he lowers his mouth to mine and kisses me breathlessly. His request for patience echoes in my mind. I've been waiting for years. True, I shared my interest in him, but I'm not confident Alden understands the reality of pining for years. Despite my limited and not recent experience, I want to tear off his clothes and explore every dip and curve I feel beneath his shirt. Previously unmatched blissful sensations zip through me. When he kisses me, the world around me ceases to exist. I'm looking forward to spending more time with Alden.

He breaks our connection after a light kiss to my forehead. There aren't enough words for the sweetness and swoon attached to that move. "Good night, Carly."

"Bye." I key open my front door and step inside. Alden doesn't leave until the locks are engaged. With happiness and hope for the future, at least personally, I turn in for the night.

CHAPTER THIRTEEN

ALDEN

The drive from Carly's home isn't long. You would think my emotions would be in check. The opposite is true. I'm a mess.

Immediately upon arriving, I strip off my clothes at the edge of the pool and dive in. It seems my therapy plan continues despite Carly being on my mind. Honestly, she's found a way to surround the pesky organ beneath my ribcage as well. Handling that is where I seem to be suspended right now.

Asha had an innate ability to make every person she encountered feel special. I tap the trim at the far end of the pool and shift to Alicia. My daughter would be hanging out with the guys at the station to learn about the family business. Would she have followed in those footsteps? Perhaps. But she would know it was an option. These thoughts come faster than usual. I haven't even finished one complete lap yet.

I span two lengths of the pool before landing on the positive aspect of my day. Carly. She has been invading my thoughts more and more. Truthfully, I don't want that to change. Reconciling the shift in my mind is harder than I imagined it would be. She makes me smile when we're apart. A random memory of the moments I spent with her brings me joy. I resolve to ask her to the ball when I see her for dinner.

A few miles later, I haul myself out of the water. Probably should have sooner. I shower and slip into bed. Before I close my eyes, I send her a text.

Me: Sweet dreams, Carly.

I hoped for an answer, but it was only after I sent the message that I realize the time. It's been a few hours, and she's likely sound asleep.

Bright and early the next morning, I see Foster and Madden in the staff lounge. They are set to leave soon.

"Morning, Rhodes," Foster greets me.

I nod, continue to my office, and close the door behind me. When I sit at my desk, I notice a few messages on my desk. The one from the chief stands out.

Picking up the phone, I call his office.

"York Fire. Chief Bertoni speaking."

My nerves are off the charts when I reply, "Morning. Lieutenant Rhodes returning your message."

"Captain. Great to hear from you."

A combination of giddiness and sadness wraps around me. "I'm sorry. What?"

Chief laughs. "I gather your uncle didn't share. Your promotion is official. This call is to set up an appointment for your new contract tomorrow and prepare the house for a promotion ceremony this week."

A heads-up from my boss/uncle would've been nice. Hell, a note on my desk could've done the job. Pride and nervousness zip through me. "Thank you, sir. Does one on Friday afternoon work for you?"

"Yes. I'll see you then. Please review your new contract and get any errors or amendments to my office by close of business Thursday. My admin will send it over shortly if she hasn't already."

I move my mouse and input my password. Then I scan the contents of my inbox. "It arrived about ten minutes ago. I'll read through it ASAP."

"Congratulations, Alden. Your father would be proud."

"Thank you. I'll see you then."

My first inclination isn't to reach out to my mother or sister. I want to share with Carly and see if she's available.

I pull out my phone and notice she responded to my message from last night. I recently changed her contact in my phone from her full name to just her first.

Carly: Thank you. Morning.

Me: Will you give me a call during your lunch break?

This time she answers instantly.

Carly: Sure. Are you okay?

Me: All good things. Talk later. xoxo

Carly: Looking forward to it. xoxo

A knock on my door draws my attention away from my phone.

"Come in."

Collings is a solid firefighter. He's tall and lanky but diligent about procedure. "Hey LT."

"What's up?"

He shifts his weight from his toes to his heels. "I wanted to confirm that I'm off for the next few weeks. With Cap retiring…."

My uncle read in the crew in one of his last few shifts. Collings's girlfriend is due to deliver their second child soon. Before answering, I pull up the schedule for the next few months. "You're all set. Cap has you as a floater beginning your next shift."

That means Collings is basically an extra body until his child is born. Then we have enough staff for him to be out.

"Great. Thanks."

"You're welcome." I pause and then add, "We are having a visit from the Chief on Friday. Can you gather the guys and tidy up the house?"

"On it," he answers and disappears.

Thankfully, the morning is devoid of calls. I tackle my inbox and what I plan to say at the ceremony. Just before lunchtime, I reach out and share the news with my family now that it's officially happening.

"Good morning, Alden."

"Hey, Mom. Are you free on Friday at one?"

"I can be. What's up?"

"Uncle Stephon put in his packet for retirement. Chief is swearing me in at the house."

"Congratulations! Your father would be so proud of you and the leader you've grown into. I'll be there. Have you spoken with Essie yet?"

"No, she's next on the list." A niggle in the back of my mind emerges that I reached out to Carly first. Despite my worries about moving forward and falling for someone other than my wife, I'm only slightly uncomfortable.

"I'll call her. Perhaps there is someone else you might want to invite?" my mother suggests.

Yes. Very much so. "What are you talking about?"

"Our hometown is small, and nothing is private. You should be aware of this fact. Mrs. Brundel shared that you have purchased flowers on more than one occasion recently. I didn't get flowers from you nor did your sister."

Damn it! So much for slow, steady, and on our terms. "There might be."

"I won't pry, but it's time for you to be happy, Alden."

"Thank you." Her deference to my privacy is appreciated especially since it's a far stretch from her comfort zone.

I can hear the pride in her voice when she replies, "I'll see you at the ceremony."

Rather than stew, I check on the cleaning progress and ask to speak with McCormick in my office.

"What's up, LT?" he asks, taking a seat in the chair across from my desk. Luckily, I have an actual office. Most of the other houses have combination areas for officers, like on the show *Chicago Fire.* There, Lieutenant Casey has a semi-private sleeping quarters and a desk. I have a mostly private bunk and an office. I share the details of my promotion with McCormick. He'll be the most senior at the house and likely handle most of my current duties.

"Congrats!"

I acknowledge him and ask, "Have you taken the exam to rise up in the ranks?"

He shakes his head.

"Are you interested?"

He's a thinner guy, and he shifts noticeably in the chair. Before answering, he sits up perfectly straight as if to project the importance of his reply. "Frankly, no."

I mask my surprise better than I thought possible. It would've been nice for Uncle Stephon to inform me that I would need to find a new team member right away. "May I ask why?"

"I don't want to give up fighting fires and protecting the people of our town. No offense but delegating at a scene is not who I am. Rushing into the fray is." McCormick answers quickly and succinctly. I believe him.

His position makes sense. Firefighting was a stepping stone for me. Leading a house was always my dream. It was another aspect of attending college. Along with swimming for another four years, I earned a degree in fire science. It covered all facets of the job, including investigation, fire suppression, and commanding a team. "I understand. I have tasked Collings with cleaning the house for the chief's visit. Please assist him."

"Will do. Congrats again," he offers and leaves my office.

Anxiously, I watch the clock tick to her lunch hour without a call. The protective guy in me yearns to reach out and check on her. The widower in a budding relationship for the first time in years doesn't want to push too hard. The realist wins though. She's a first responder and is likely embroiled in a trauma or dealing with the potential strike of her employees.

I grab my cell phone to reach out to my uncle.

"Hey, Alden."

I divulge my conversation with McCormick and ask for his advice and suggestions on filling the position.

"Sutter from the 20th and Bryce from the 15th are the best options. You might want to contact their captains to schedule meetings."

Inwardly, I grumble. I don't even have the job officially, and I'm doing his work. "Will do."

The tones ring out, and I hurry to the engine. Interestingly, Reed beats me there. I hear the call "Motor vehicle crash into restaurant at 2 Main Street."

That address is a popular eatery in the village. They serve breakfast and lunch. The tourist population has steadily increased over the last few weeks. It could also mean numerous injuries, not only to patrons but to people on the street.

"Engine 4 responding. Requesting YPD send additional units for traffic control and rerouting."

Dispatch replies, "Copy."

When we arrive, the scene is chaotic. Cars are parked in the road unable to move, and the drivers are standing outside their vehicles. As I hop off the truck and approach on foot, I note a sedan has crashed through the outdoor seating area and into the building. The majority of the car is inside the structure. Before walking to the responding police units, I direct my team to prepare for extrication and assess the situation. Then I locate the first unit from YPD. *Great, Piper.* "Afternoon, Montgomery and Greyson."

Piper swivels toward my voice. "You?"

Greyson is a younger officer on the force. He's fit and average looking, although he has a reputation among the ladies in town as a player.

I don't read into Piper's response. The tone is disdainful. Right now, I don't care. Opting out of a second date with her was absolutely the right move. I take in the area and note we are second to arrive.

I direct them. "Please close the road above the restaurant there." I point to the intersection at Main and Freeman. "Then turn those two cars around. Once completed, close the top of Beach Street to traffic."

Greyson replies, "Roger."

Piper grouses but complies.

"Rhodes." I hear my name and turn to find Captain Ramirez approaching. He's coming from the far side of Short Sands Beach.

"My team is assessing, and I directed Greyson and Montgomery to close the roads," I share.

"Good. I'll work this part. You see what you can do about the occupants of the vehicle and the building. Ransom and Penn are on scene. Secondary units are stuck behind the traffic."

I nod and hustle to the front of the building.

"Penn, update," I demand. Séamus Penn is an experienced EMT and also a local.

"Teenage driver has no recollection of the accident. Laceration on her forehead and claims inability to control her right leg. Front passenger is unconscious, no response when called, and no clear line of sight. Backseat passenger is trapped but indicates she's otherwise uninjured."

I turn to my crew. "Madden and Foster, crib the vehicle so we can extricate the victims. Reed and McCormick, check the rear for access and report before entering.

"On it," Reed answers. They hustle around the building.

The traffic congestion eases. Collings rolls the engine as close to the scene as possible, followed tightly by a second ambulance. Vaughn and Pascal exit and hurry over with supplies and a stretcher.

My phone vibrates in my pocket. *Carly.* I resist the urge to check the message. It's difficult, but I pull it off. Normally, it's on silent to avoid the same while on a call like now.

"Lieutenant," comes over the radio.

"Go, Reed."

"There is access in the rear. It's locked, but we can cut it off the hinges."

"Roger. Get into the building and assess."

"On it," he replies.

The crew at the front have secured the car and assisted the driver and front passenger. Both are en route to the hospital.

Penn waves me closer. "Rhodes, we can't get to the third victim this way. Check it out."

I crouch and look into the vehicle. "What's your name?"

"Junie."

"Hi. I'm Alden. My friend here says you're trapped but unhurt, right?"

"Yes."

"Ok—"

The radio crackles, and I hear, "Lieutenant."

"Give me a second, Junie. Go, Reed."

"I have three minor injuries to workers, one serious arm injury, and a missing patron."

Crap! "Penn, send medical assistance to the rear of building." He talks to his crew over the radio while I return my attention to Junie. "Can you find the latch near the top of the seat?"

"To lower it?" she asks.

"Yes, exactly. This car is newer and is equipped with a way to open the trunk from the inside."

"Okay." Her voice is shaky, but I hear her shifting.

I press the button on my radio, "Foster, move to the rear of the car and prepare for the third victim to emerge from the trunk."

"Roger," he replies over the radio.

"I can't see anything. It's dark."

"Take a breath, Junie. The handle will glow in the dark." I inform her.

A second later, I hear a pop and light streams into the trunk. Immediately, cheers erupt in front of the building.

Penn and I emerge. I reallocate resources to assist Reed and Collings, then catch up with Captain Ramirez.

"I have an update." I share Reed's assessment and ask him to push the gathered onlookers back.

"Understood. No problem. Smart move using the trunk latch."

"Thanks."

After my discussion with William, I join my crew. Vaughn and Pascal are moving the injured to the rig. Reed provides a better update when I reach him.

"Rhodes, the missing patron was just located in the restroom. Debris blocked his exit, and the equipment drowned out his pleas for help. Victim has minor lacerations from attempting to break down the door himself."

"Roger. Let's get these people to York Memorial and secure the building."

Relieved that the patron was located, we finish the call and return to the station. After stowing my gear, I finally look at my phone and notice a text from Carly.

Carly: I got caught up with Willa and the board. Please reach out when you're free later tonight.

Carly: I heard about the call near the beach. Dinner for you and the guys is on the way from Vocaturra's. xoxo

Me: You didn't have to do that.

Carly: I would cook myself, but I'm terrible for large groups. Hell, I'm not a great bet for only me.

I can't contain the smile or laugh from her words.

Me: Doubtful. Please accept appreciation from me and the guys. I'll call you later. xoxo

Carly: Looking forward to it.

No sooner did we finish texting, and the food arrives.

"Lieutenant!" Reed shouts from the kitchen.

Shaking my head, I follow his voice. "Yes?"

"We got a delivery. There are tons of sandwiches and chips and drinks from Voc's in here," he shares.

"Great. Is there a card or note?" I ask.

Foster frowns. "Who cares. We didn't have to cook dinner after a tough call."

They check the bags and find a note on the bottom of the receipt. "Thank you for your service to our community."

I select a sandwich and chips before hiding in my office. I settle in my chair and dig in. I glance at the clock and realize she isn't home yet. I appreciate she reached out and she's fine. I'm edgy waiting to share my huge news with her.

CHAPTER FOURTEEN

CARLY

When the initial patients were announced, I knew it would be a long and difficult call for Alden and his crew. Without overthinking how it might be received, I zipped away to my office for fifteen minutes and placed the order.

I've donated a meal to Landry's house before. However, today is the first time I did it for relationship reasons, not altruism or community support. The schedule of a firefighter isn't an easy one. I'm used to it because of my brother. We work around his as best we can. Providing dinner is the least I could do.

Willa and I exit the hospital at the same time.

She looks left and right to make sure we're alone. "Spill, sister." Willa is asking about my date. We've had more discussion than I care to admit about the status of the contract and the potential strike. The board moved a little but not enough, in my opinion. I'm scheduled to update the nursing staff early next week.

I can't stop the smile from widening on my face. "We had a great time at the game."

"But?" she asks.

"It isn't a but exactly. We're taking a slow and steady approach. It might kill me though."

Willa raises an eyebrow.

I continue, "I have wanted to test our compatibility for years. The more time I spend with him, the more the urgency to get him naked increases. Seeing if his abs are carved from marble is high on my to-do list right about now."

Willa laughs. "The waiting only makes the first coupling better. Trust me. Luca and I went from waffling near shortstop to a home run." Only one of my besties would use a baseball analogy.

I close my eyes and force the image of Alden in my mind to linger a bit. "Thanks." We hug and go our separate ways.

Before leaving the lot, I place a delivery order for my favorite Thai food. With the low hum of country music on in the background, I drive home. Soon after I arrive, the doorbell rings. With my panang curry and chicken satay in hand, I take a seat on my rear patio. It's still warm, and the sun hasn't set yet.

Overall, work today wasn't too bad, at least not physically. My staff likely won't be happy when I share the potential shortfall in the board's offer.

Without looking at the caller, I answer my phone.

"Hello."

"Hey, Carly. Are you busy?"

I swallow my food and reply, "Hi, Alden. Just finishing dinner."

He pauses for a bit too long for my liking. Worry and concern ricochet through me.

"Is everything okay?"

"Yes. The Chief called me today. My promotion is now official."

"Congratulations!" Pride blooms within me. We may be new as a couple but he's been working his way up the ranks for years.

Unlike his normal smooth self, Alden blurts, "Can you take the day off on Friday and come to my promotion ceremony? I asked for a slower pace. If you aren't ready to go that kind of public I—"

"Breathe, Alden." I purposely wait to add more until I hear a few solid inhales through the phone. "I'll be there if you're ready for me to be."

Before he utters another word, I get a video request. After I accept, his chiseled face appears on my screen.

"I wanted to see your face when I answered."

Fear swirls around my heart. He wouldn't pull the invitation back, right?

Alden adds, "Honestly…."

I nod, urging him to continue. Our past requires it.

"… I'm unsure of my readiness for our family, friends, and townspeople to weigh in just yet. However, I know another promotion ceremony in my career is unlikely. More so because I don't have any desire to be battalion chief. I want to share it with you. You… we… our potential is…."

"I'm hesitant to share our relationship widely as well. The irony isn't lost on me. My group meddles in the love lives of our friends and coworkers. I'll be there."

"Thank you."

"Of course."

We chat for a little while about my day before the tones sound at the house.

"I'll message you when we get back. Good night, Carly."

"Be safe. I'll see you for dinner tomorrow."

"Always."

At the beginning of his career, Landry used to text me when he went out on a call and when he returned. Slowly, over the years, they have ended. My brother did it to placate me. I appreciate that Alden realizes my need to know he's safe after a call. I clean up my dinner trash, lock up, and snuggle into my bed. Thanks to Scarlett, I have a new book to read. Well, it isn't recently published, but I started *The Summer House* by James Patterson a few days ago. It's engaging.

One hundred pages later, I check my phone and worry there hasn't been a message from Alden. Instead of disregarding my feelings, I dig into them. I care about him more than I think I should at this point. Diving deeper, I don't care. For the first time—probably ever—I'm happy in a relationship. I thought Kenneth was a good guy. It turns out a man who transfers from southern Florida to Maine is running from something. That is one of the main reasons sharing makes me nervous. I don't want others weighing in. I know my besties can, and Rafael too. However, at least as far as Scarlett and Willa go, they respect my boundaries. I'm grateful.

Setting my worry aside, I set an alarm and go to sleep. The next thing I know it's morning again.

When I check my phone before for work, I find a message from Alden a few hours ago.

Alden M. Rhodes: Back safely at the house. See you tonight.

Me: Can't wait. What is for dinner?

It's barely breakfast, but who cares.

Alden M. Rhodes: Don't know yet. Have a great day.

Me: I'll try.

I should know better. Thinking about the end of a shift only makes it feel longer.

The ambulance bay has been a revolving door since my arrival. No rest for the weary, I suppose. Aside from that, I have two callouts for the day shift. I have been elbow-deep with these patients rather than supervising. I don't mind it, but I would have preferred a heads-up.

By the end of my shift, I'm tired, cranky, and starving. As much as I push my staff to take a break and eat, I didn't follow my own advice today. I've been surviving on a Nutri-Grain bar and water. The bright spot is a delicious meal is waiting for me at Alden's. Spending time with him alone will be nice as well.

The picture floats in my mind. That is until I reach my office and check my messages.

Alden M. Rhodes: Wanted to let you know. My sister and nephews are here using the pool.

Bubble burst. A wave of uncertainty tumbles over me. I assume Essie will be there on Friday for the ceremony. While my mind whirls, I read the next message.

Alden M. Rhodes: I still want to see you tonight.

I consider my options. I don't want to cancel on him either.

Me: I'll stop home for my swimsuit and then come over. Work for you?

Alden M. Rhodes: Thank you. See you soon.

After my tiring day, a leisurely swim might be nice. Plus sharing our relationship tonight with Essie and her sons will eliminate some of the pressure for the ceremony on Friday.

I pull into my driveway and hurry inside. When I open my drawer to locate my bathing suit, I realize neither are appropriate, considering the attendees this evening. I grab the two-piece bikini that covers the most and a tank top. Without overthinking more, I get back into my car and drive to Alden's.

As I'm about to knock on the door, it swings open. My gorgeous... my? *Yes.* I'm owning it. My gorgeous man greets me with a sweet kiss that barely takes the edge off my weariness from the workday and my anxiety in sharing our coupling.

"Don't worry. You already met Essie. Halston and Henry will be polite and then splash you mercilessly."

"Noted. Let's go." I set the gift bag on the couch and follow him outside.

Silence falls over the backyard when we emerge from the house.

"Carly. How nice to see you again," Essie greets me. There isn't surprise in her voice, which makes me wonder. I don't ponder it for long.

"You as well."

A tall young boy, about eight, runs around the pool. "Hi, I'm Halston. Are you Uncle Alden's girlfriend?" His question is directed at me.

"Yes." Alden's deep, sexy voice answers for me.

"She's pretty," he states, looking up at his uncle.

"I noticed, bud," Alden replies.

The other boy, who is clearly younger, slowly approaches from my right. I crouch and wave.

"Hi, I'm Carly. What's your name?"

He extends his tiny hand to me. "Henry. Pleased to meet you."

Awww! I take it and reply, "You too."

Seemingly satisfied with our meet-cute, the boys jump back into the pool.

Alden ushers me to the lounger along the wall. "I need to finish dinner. Will you be okay out here?"

"Girlfriend, huh?"

He tilts his head with worry. "Easiest explanation for him."

"Good point. It's accurate though."

"It is. I'm not a fan that the first time you swim here will be without me."

"You and I can jump in after we eat. Just the two of us." My intention wasn't to lace my words with innuendo. Oh well.

Alden leans closer and whispers, "Looking forward to it." He turns to leave but then retreats and adds, "I really want to kiss you senseless, but we need to talk more."

"Will we… after dinner. Go. I'll be fine."

He hesitates again but returns to the kitchen. Whatever he planned to cook wasn't easily switched to the grill. I toe off my shoes and wiggle out of my shorts. I'm still edgy about my bathing suit. Would I wear it to the beach without a tank top? Yes. The mere fact I considered the shirt was enough to keep it on. My body image is good, but it isn't akin to a runway supermodel. I'll wear whatever I want though.

With the black tank knotted at the small of my back, I walk down the steps into the pool. The water temperature is spot on. I shouldn't be surprised. The boys are completely oblivious to my presence. Essie has her eyes trained on Henry and Halston. I'm confident Alden taught them to swim, but I appreciate her diligence for their safety.

Once I reach the bottom, I push off the floor and glide to the deep end. A few laps later, I sit on the steps and watch the boys play. It isn't long before Alden exits the house with a platter of food.

"Come on, guys. Let's eat."

It's only then that I noticed the table was already set. His nephews throw towels around their shoulders and grab a chair.

"What did you make?" Henry asks.

Alden grins at him. "Chicken with loads of veggies and pasta." He takes a seat beside me.

The expected "Ewwww" doesn't come. They fill their plates and eat in silence.

Essie wastes no time digging for information. "How long have you been dating my brother?"

I can't suppress the smile. "Not long. We're both private and wanted to wade in slowly."

His sister laughs heartily. "You know our mother and the ladies of this town. Hell, you're one of them."

I shake my head. "It was a fool's errand, I suppose."

Alden squeezes my thigh beneath the table to get my attention and nods tightly.

Henry and Halston are refilling their plates before I'm halfway done with my first serving. Young and hungry would be an understatement. When they finish, the boys and Essie bring their dishes inside.

When they return, his sister says, "It's nice to see you, Carly. We're going to head home. They have school tomorrow." Summer break is rapidly approaching for them.

Groans erupt from the boys. With a sharp look from Essie, they pipe down and gather their stuff. Henry, Halston, and Alden fly through a complicated handshake. I earn a single high five from both of them.

Well-wishes and good nights echo as they hurry down the front steps.

Alden turns to face me, and I blurt the question that has been on my mind since his text. "Does she frequently show up like that?"

"Yes. More so in the spring and summer months. Before, I didn't feel the need to set limits with my sister and my house."

I shrug. They could unknowingly crash future dates.

He continues, "I asked Essie to make sure I didn't have plans or company going forward."

"Thank you. How long until... Glad... Mama Rhodes knows?"

He draws me close, kisses the top of my wet hair, and chuckles. "She probably already does. Not sure what to call her, huh?"

I shake my head against his chest. "Not at all. It's kind of comical."

"Meaning?"

"I have a well-established relationship with your mom, and it has nothing to do with you. It's slightly weird actually."

"Not to me. I get you aren't sure what name to use, which makes sense. Otherwise, I have no concerns that she'll love you. She gave you her group. Her opinion of you is stellar, without question." *No pressure.* "Either way, only my opinion matters. Mom and Essie accepting us together is merely a bonus."

"Thank you."

"Ready to jump in with me?"

I hesitate inwardly for a hot second. *He means in the pool.* "Yes."

He takes my hand and leads me to the edge of the pool again. "Before we do…," he pauses too long for my liking.

"Just say it," I urge him.

"What's with the tank top?"

I purse my lips and choose my words carefully before answering. "I wasn't sure… I felt like my swimsuit was too revealing for your guests, so I covered up a bit."

"I see." He adds nothing else before diving into the deep end. "Come on."

At his urging, I slide into the water at the midpoint of the pool. I'm straddling the demarcation for the shallow and deep ends.

Alden glides through the water and cages me in against the wall. "Thank you for coming even with my family here. I know we decided to keep us to ourselves for a bit."

"You're welcome. That isn't working out very well. Lacey and Hagen saw our attraction. Plus, joining you on Friday will put a spotlight on our relationship anyway."

"True."

"A few days sooner and a lot less people at once is fine. Besides, York Elementary is a hotbed of gossip."

He laughs deeply and then lowers his mouth to mine. Each time Alden kisses me, the world disappears. I don't hear the sounds of nature or the pool filter kicking on. Only the sound of my heart pounding in my ears and the unmatched sensations of his touch are noticeable. Common sense and yearning brawl for supremacy in my mind and body. I haven't felt this much from a kiss… ever.

His next question pulls me out of my thoughts briefly. "Was your only concern my nephews?"

Shivers run down my spine despite the warm water. "Yes."

"Good." He drags his palms down my sides and around my back before unknotting the shirt. "I appreciate your consideration of decency, but they're gone." He lifts the sopping material over my head and reclaims my lips. His big hands guide my legs around his waist. My torso is mostly above the waterline.

It's impossible to miss his response to me. It's been a long time since a man has been this close to me outside of a hug. Words fail to adequately describe the decadent ribbons of pleasure coursing through me, and we're still mostly clothed. What will being with him do to me? I'm on the verge of losing my mind from his hands and mouth alone.

A few sultry kisses later, he adds a sliver of space between us. "You're stunning."

Alden travels along my jawline and down my neck. Containing my whimper is an epic failure. My fingers dig into his shoulders as I try to hold myself up a bit. Alden draws the strap of my black bikini top along my arm.

The warmth of his mouth on my puckered nipple sends a zip of pleasure southward.

He secures me against his body and walks to the stairs. Setting me on the second step, Alden resumes lavishing attention to my breasts equally. Heat pools between my thighs. This spot allows me to explore him. I drag my hand over the rock-hard planes of his chest and trace the divots of his impressive eight-pack of abs. His frame is insane. I dip my hand into his trunks and stroke him.

"Carly," he rasps, mirroring my movements.

"Need me to stop?"

Instead of answering, he slides his fingers between my thighs. Without finesse, he pushes a digit inside me and matches my evenly paced strokes along his impressive shaft.

"Alden." Never before have I felt unparalleled bliss from a man's hands. My inner walls tense and pulse as he lengthens in my hold. Pressure intensifies in my lower belly. Flutters swirl and increase until I'm shaking with pleasure. Alden's hand moves furiously as waves roar forward.

Somehow I manage to maintain my grip on him while reveling in new heights of ecstasy.

"Don't stop, Carly," Alden grits out.

Two deep strokes later, he explodes in my grasp. Our gazes meet as we catch our breath.

"I will never look at a pool the same again," he whispers near my ear.

"Me neither." I slip my hand out of his swim trunks.

He shakes his head. "We didn't think this through."

"Worth it."

"Absolutely." He brushes his lips across mine and slowly withdraws his hand from my bikini bottom. "I have an outdoor shower where we can rinse off a bit." He stands and helps me to my feet. I wobble slightly, but he doesn't call me out. If he realized the magnitude of this encounter, he might be worried for me. The last time a man made me shake in a good way was too long ago.

The outdoor shower is glorious. We rinse off, wrap up in huge, soft, towels, and pad inside.

CHAPTER FIFTEEN

CARLY

I feel the caress of Alden's lips on top of my head. Then I hear my name. "Carly."

"Hmmm?"

"You need to get moving or you'll be late for work."

I groan and mumble against his bare skin. "I don't wanna."

"So don't."

I lift my head, and look into his soulful eyes. "You don't have anything to do today?"

"I do but I would rather spend my time with you."

Leaning closer I kiss Alden lightly. "I would love to call in and spend the day with you. I can't. I have to finish the proposal for the staff so I can be at the ceremony tomorrow."

"It's no problem. I just wanted you to know."

"Same."

I twist and hang my legs off the edge of his bed. As I pad to the en suite bathroom, I ask, "Got a spare toothbrush?"

"No. I only buy them when I need them. Use mine, and I'll pick one up for you today."

"Okay."

"How much time you have?"

I peek at my smartwatch. "Fifteen minutes. Why?"

He hurries over to me for a kiss and rushes out of his bedroom.

Ten minutes later, I join him in the kitchen. "I'll wash this and bring it back." I tug on his shirt.

"Keep it. I probably have a dozen."

"I need an exchange program then."

I turn to face him fully with a bagel and tea prepared for me.

"A what?"

"You have tea?"

He pauses and replies, "Yes. I bought tea to have it on hand for you."

I can't conceal the huge smile from widening on my face. "No man has…."

"Happy to be the first to care for you properly." He hugs me close. "What do you mean, an exchange program?"

My lips pull into a thin, straight line. "The hoodie doesn't smell like you anymore mostly because I use it daily at home."

He laughs. "Okay. I can do that."

"I don't want to go, but…." With another all-too-short kiss, I hurry out the front door. By the time I reach my house, I have approximately thirty minutes to get ready and drive to work. The commute is fifteen. *I can do this!* As I walk into my home, I'm stripping off my clothes. I take the fastest shower of my life and dress. Meanwhile my phone is pinging with texts.

I ignore them and hustle out the door dressed in scrubs and a cardigan because it's freezing in my office. I plan to keep myself sequestered in there as much as possible today. Frankly, I don't have a choice. The board provided their last and final offer, and I must polish it up and get it to my staff. I'm looking forward to tomorrow and don't want anything to mess it up for Alden.

When I arrive, I use the parking garage entrance to avoid chatting. I'm successful in both getting to work on time and making it into my office without unnecessary chitchat. As my computer wakes, I check my messages.

Alden M. Rhodes: Can I make dinner at your place tonight?

Me: Are you implying I can't prepare my own food?

Alden M. Rhodes: Who, me?

Alden M. Rhodes: Also, yes.

Me: Very funny. I can cook, just not well. Yes, I would like to see you.

Alden M. Rhodes: I'll meet you there. Have a great day. xoxo.

Me: You too.

I spend the morning writing and then editing the counterproposal to the staff. I sneak down to the cafeteria to purchase lunch. I'm almost back to my office when I get paged to the emergency room. When I arrive, I note the board is clear, and there's nothing for me to handle until I hear the shouting. I look up and see Janie and Mik nearly nose to nose.

"How long has that been going on?" I ask Katia, who is manning the reception desk."

"A solid ten minutes," she replies.

I acknowledge her and stash my food. I diffuse a heated disagreement between Janie and Mik about the potential responses from the board.

"Turning on each other won't work. I will have the counterproposal ready by the end of the day."

"Really?" Mik asks.

"Yes."

Janie adds, "Sorry, Mikel. I'm not a great person when I'm anxious. I truly don't want to do a job search right now."

Mik replies, "No worries." They fist-bump and return to their duties. Arguably it is in my job description to handle team strife. Until this unionization threat, I never had to.

Katia extends my lunch to me with an appreciative smile. Before more discord erupts, I leave quickly.

Rather than eat, I go to the NICU to snuggle away my anger and dismay for the state of my job.

Scarlett makes a beeline for me as soon as I badge onto the floor. We hug and walk into the nursery.

"Hey! Rough day already?"

I drop my head. A few minutes later, I'm gowned up and holding a new preemie. Ivy was born at thirty weeks gestation after a car accident caused a placental abruption. Mom and Dad are recovering as well.

Scarlett whispers, "Can you share?"

I shrug and parse out my response. "My team is ornery and edgy. It's understandable. I just diffused a disagreement between Mik and Janie."

"Aren't their kids dating?"

"Yes, which makes the arguing even more intense."

"Work pause…."

A work pause means we're besties only right now. I'm not drafting an agreement that will affect her salary and personal time off. "Granted."

She leans in uber close and whispers, "There's going to be an opening on this floor very soon. The supervising nurse got engaged and will be leaving due to her fiancé's job."

My heart tumbles, and my eyes light up. "When?"

"She may have already put in her notice. If I were you, I would go see Willa when you're done soaking up the baby juju."

I exhale slowly. "You're the best ever!"

Scarlett winks at me. "I know. Love you."

"Love you too."

Thirty minutes later, I take her advice rather than return straight to my office. Honestly, the proposal only needs a once-over. I didn't want to share that with my team members though. Plus, I'm seriously grateful Alden invited me tomorrow, and I won't be here when they are stewing over the provisions.

I knock on Willa's office door, hoping she's available.

"Come in," Willa responds. Her office is much nicer than mine. It should be, given her responsibilities are far greater.

"Carly. Hey."

That doesn't sound good. "Hi. What's wrong?"

"I know why you're here."

I frown. "You do?"

"You want an extension for the counterproposal," she states.

"Absolutely not. It's done, minus another review."

Willa tilts her head in interest. "Okay. What can I help you with?"

I take a seat. "Work pause…."

"Granted."

I continue, "A little red birdie mentioned there may be an opening for my dream job."

She purses her lips. "Yes. It will be posted next week."

Glee shoots through me. "Are there any other internal candidates who beat my qualifications?"

Willa wrinkles her nose. "Exceed… no. Comes close… yes."

I wrack my brain trying to figure out who it is. Only one person jumps to mind, and frankly, she's older and nearing retirement. "Okay. I'll look for the posting and apply. Perhaps my closest competition is willing to take my position?"

"Maybe. How is Alden?"

I can't stop the warmth that zips through me, and my friend calls me out.

"I gather things are going well from your rosy cheeks and shifting in the chair."

"They are. I'm cautiously optimistic. We have a few aspects to iron out, but they're big."

"You haven't… yet?"

"No. We came close, but my experience is a lot to handle for a man of his worth. Plus, he isn't aware the reason I want to switch departments is him."

"All you can do is be honest. Alden is an exceptional man, and he'll understand."

"He is. Saying the words out loud again is something else." Only Scarlett and Willa know about the sexual assault in my past. Sharing with Alden isn't going to be easy but must be done.

"You need to, though."

I agree. "I will. Hopefully soon."

"About the NICU too."

I close my eyes and will myself not to tear up. "After his promotion ceremony, I'll tell him."

"Good. Now, go finish that report so you can be off tomorrow in peace."

With a stupid grin on my face which is more for Alden than completing the proposal, I thank her and leave. With so many thoughts on my mind, I press the "do not disturb" button on my office phone. Before I do the same with my personal phone, I note a text from my brother.

Landry: Are you free tomorrow after the ceremony?

Me: How do you know I'm coming?

Landry: Rhodes mentioned he invited you.

Me: Oh. I was going take him to dinner to celebrate.

Landry: Maybe me and my girlfriend could tag along?

Me: I'll talk to him and get back to you.

Landry: Sounds good. Are you two....?

Me: No comment.... Yet.

It's stupid for me not to admit it. My presence tomorrow will scream volumes to everyone present. He also called me his girlfriend last night.

Landry: LOL.

I silence my cellphone and go through the paperwork twice more. To me, it's a fair deal. The staff asked for ten dollars over two years with two full days off. This final offer from the board proposes six dollars over three years with one full day off. The new contract doesn't affect me, but I would take it.

I finish up, check the recipient list, and schedule the email to be sent precisely thirty minutes before the deadline. I'll make sure it goes out, but this allows me not to stress more with the wording. I tap my finger on my desk until the email disappears from my scheduled folder. Verifying the message was indeed sent with appropriate attachments, I gather my things and exit to the parking garage.

Thankfully, I make it safely off hospital property without running into any staff members. When I arrive home, I find Alden sitting on my front porch. Happiness swirls in my chest at the sight of him. Is this normal? If so, I'm in.

He strides to the edge of the driveway to greet me. "Hi, beautiful."

Once I'm on my feet, he kisses me like the world is going to end. Then again, his lips on mine feels monumental every single time. Only after I'm breathless do I greet him. "Hi."

"How was your day?" he asks while taking my tote off my hands.

"Not too bad. I sent the best and final offer and learned about an opening for my dream job."

He leads me to the porch. "Dream job? Care to share?" While I unlock the door, he grabs two bags near the chair.

"I will discuss over dinner. What's in there?" I ask.

"I'm confident your fridge is basically bare. It's ingredients for dinner."

"You aren't wrong."

He laughs. "I know. Why don't you change while I get started?"

I frown. "How do you… never mind." This man never ceases to amaze me with his attention to detail. He came over once after work for the initial softball meeting. Thankfully, the game is next weekend. Nearly all the final details are ironed out.

When I return to the kitchen, my scrubs have been replaced with leggings, a fitted tank, and an open-back workout shirt. "Can I help?"

Alden is deep into cooking. "If you want to get plates and drinks, sure. This will be done in about ten minutes."

"Impressive. Hot-as-hell fire captain and you make a delicious, healthy meal in twenty minutes."

"Thanks."

He plates seasoned chicken over orzo with cherry tomatoes and asparagus. After a few bites, Alden says, "Tell me about the job."

"I always wanted to be a NICU nurse, but there hasn't been an opening. Scarlett shared that the supervising nurse is leaving."

Alden frowns. "You were on that floor today."

I set down my fork and exhale slowly. "Since I started at York Memorial, I spend my lunches or whenever I'm having a rough day loving on the preemies."

"Oh."

"It's a way for me to help even though it isn't my job."

He takes a sip of his iced tea and asks, "Why preemies?"

Sharing my inclination to heal the tiniest of humans should be terrifying. It isn't with him. That's telling. "In nursing school, I found preemies were not only a huge challenge but also massive triumphs if medical technology could carry them to full gestation age with minimal deficits. They fascinated me. I did an extended program in Boston during school. After...." I reach out and cover his hand with mine.

He looks straight at me. Perhaps he realizes the rest of this story is about him, but maybe he doesn't.

"When we didn't save your daughter...." I swallow hard and risk looking into his deep brown eyes. "I scoured the job opportunities for a NICU nurse spot for a few years. I even considered moving out of York Beach."

"Why?"

I swipe away the tear that rolled down my cheek. "I wanted to give her a chance. I voted to try but was summarily overruled due to lack of experience and a host of other reasons that echo in my mind each time I help out upstairs."

Alden is stunned speechless. I expect him to get up and walk out of my home and never return. A few full minutes pass without anything other than him breathing and staring at our linked hands.

I give him the out. "I will understand if you need to leave and not see me anymore. This can't be easy to hear. It would suck, I won't lie, but I'll get over it… eventually."

A scowl appears on his gorgeous face. "Why would I do that? You didn't make the deciding vote. Your own admission indicates you wanted to provide my baby girl a chance. I knew from the beginning you were there on the worst day of my life to date. This revelation doesn't change how I feel about you. You are becoming the most important person and my best friend. I adore you, Carly. I know it seems crazy fast, but it's true." He leans forward and kisses our linked hands.

Happiness zips through me. "I care about you too, and I agree that our feelings are more than would seem possible or acceptable at this stage."

"Good. Will you accompany me tomorrow?"

"Yes. I'll be there prepared to field the myriad of questions coming our way about our relationship status."

He grins. We finish our meal, and he leaves around ten. "I'll see you tomorrow. I meant to mention, Mama Rhodes set up a reception at Morgan's for me and my house. Will you join us?"

"Yes. Does that mean Landry would be invited?"

"Why?"

I shake my head. "He wanted to have dinner with me to meet his girlfriend. "

"An invitation was extended to him as well."

"Okay. Good night, Alden." I rise on my toes and press my lips to his. Honestly, waking up with him this morning—was that this morning?—is what I want every day. It's too soon for me to voice that sentiment. I may have shared one of my skeletons. There's one to go, and it's equally important, perhaps more so for our future.

"Sweet dreams, Carly."

I lock the door and watch him through the sidelight. Then I turn in for the night. Extra sleep will be handy in dealing with the reaction to our new relationship status tomorrow.

CHAPTER SIXTEEN

ALDEN

Diving into the deep end, I then travel a few lengths of the pool before my thoughts invade my peace. The last time I woke up with a woman in my arms, she was my wife. Carly wearing a shirt with my last name on the back should make me pause. It doesn't. The idea of marrying her doesn't invoke the urge to hurl. That's progress, significant progress. No other woman after Asha evoked such ideas in me.

After dinner, we went swimming. Sort of. We explored each other but stopped short of having sex. As much as I want to… it's been too long. It's a detail she needs to be aware of, and last night was perfect. Destroying the moment would've been tragic. We curled up on the couch and promptly fell asleep beneath a soft, cozy blanket she bought for me. I appreciate the gift more than she knows. It's for her when she's here, and I kind of love that. The gray textured blanket makes my living room more inviting and kept us warm while we snuggled on the couch.

When she woke at two, I requested she stay until morning. Carly didn't fight me. With threaded fingers, I led her to my bedroom, and we went back to sleep.

That's new for me. Perhaps I could even call it progress. Asha made every day better. I'm confident Alicia would've as well. So does Carly, I admit to myself, ignoring the stab of guilt. Alicia would be old enough for father-daughter dances at this point. Speaking of dances, I still need to ask Carly to be my date to the ball. Probably should have already. There again, she sneaks into my mind and heart. The angst of moving on dissipates more and more each minute I spend with Carly. I don't believe any other woman could've made progress as fast as her. It isn't because she's beautiful, though she is. Not only was she there, but she fought for my tiny girl. She didn't win, but she tried, and I'm eternally grateful. One positive about yesterday was learning minute details about Alicia. Nowhere in the reports did I read they discussed attempting to save her at any length. It makes sense. No grieving husband and father wants to be aware of that information. At this point, I'm indifferent to the ramifications of their decision. Over the years, I've played out every conceivable scenario, including single fatherhood. A few more laps pass before I add the positive aspect of my day: becoming part of the Rhodes fire legacy. Finishing the last one hundred meters, I walk up the stairs and towel off.

While the ceremony is for me, I don't have to organize it. For that, I'm grateful. I have a few hours before I need to leave for the house. I plan to be there by noon. Schmoozing the higher-ups in the department is not the top of my list of favorite things to do. I'll minimize it as best I can today and in the future.

While my coffee brews, there's a knock on my front door. Curious, I pad over and answer it. I'm not expecting anyone, and my family no longer visits without calling first.

"Morning," Carly greets me. She looks amazing in a red wrap dress. It accentuates her curves but is tasteful at the same time. Her hair is smooth as a sheet. Normally, it's in a twist for work.

I'm dumbstruck.

After a solid minute or more of silence, she adds, "I'm sorry. I shouldn't have just showed up… I'll see you later." Carly spins on her heels toward her sedan.

"Don't go." I finally force out.

She turns back and gazes squarely at me. "Did I misread our conversation last night?" she asks. Her voice is soft and quiet.

"No, not at all. You look fantastic, and I'm… please come in."

She slides past me, and a whiff of jasmine and vanilla teases my senses. While I should be gathering my composure, I watch her walk. Damn if I don't want to peel that dress from her body with painstaking precision. Then a stark reminder pushes forth in my mind. The resurgence of my carnal desires is great, but inexperience is still an issue, at least for me.

Regaining my ability to speak, I ask, "Would you like some tea?"

"No thanks. I've already had two cups today."

I pour myself a coffee. Taking her hand, I lead her outside onto the patio. We sit near the firepit. There's no need to turn it on. It's already warm today.

"Moving slow?" she asks. "I mean, the view is exceptional, but don't you have to get ready soon?"

"You think so?"

Her cheeks burn bright red before she answers, pointing her finger at me, "Hell yes. Those abs are insane. I mean how many men truly have that many divots?"

"Well, the same is true for you in that dress."

She puts her hands under her chin and smiles. "Why thank you."

I laugh and add, "Did we talk about when I needed to be there?"

Shaking her head, she says, "Not really, but I figured you would chat up the brass beforehand."

"I sort of did that part already. Plus," I lean closer and whisper, "I don't love that aspect of the job. I'm keeping the networking and ass-kissing to the smallest window acceptable."

She laughs softly, and the sound hits me center mass. I could listen to that sound for the rest of my life. *Whoa!* I replay those words in my mind twice before realizing I'm okay. I'm falling for her, and there is nothing I can do to slow or stop it. Then a cruel reality slaps me in the face. We need time to learn more about each other. That fact has pushed my last thought as far down as the Challenger Deep in the Mariana Trench. For now. Small steps forward are necessary for us.

"Fair enough. Do you want me to leave and meet you at the station?"

"No, please stay. I was taken aback. Not because I don't want you here, but because I might desire your company a little too much."

Her response is intriguing and on point, "Is there such a thing?"

"Maybe. Either way, we are about to become fodder for the gossip mill and soon. Are you ready for that?"

"I can handle the heat. Can you?" She winks at me.

"My training will be an asset."

"Good. What are your feelings on public displays of affection?" Carly wonders aloud.

"I'm fine with it as long as it's respectful of location and other people."

"No dancing on the firepole for me. Got it."

I turn to her with shock on my face. "Please tell me you're kidding."

"In this dress, of course. I'm thinking hand-holding, physical proximity, and small kisses are acceptable for today. Yes?"

"Proximity is required every day. Otherwise, I agree with those terms."

"Good."

We enjoy the sunshine for a while before I shower and don my fancy outfit. Carly soaks up vitamin D while she waits.

When I return clad in my dress uniform, she says, "You clean up well, Captain Rhodes."

That has a nice ring to it, especially in her sultry voice. "Not as good as you. Although, the outfit you were wearing when I showed up for the charity game planning was utterly mouthwatering."

"Remind me."

"Leggings, a fitted tank top, and a zip up. You tugged the zipper up to conceal your breasts after you invited me in."

"Well, we weren't dating then. We are now. I'll keep your preferences in mind."

"As will I."

Her eyebrows scrunch up. "Like?"

"Shirtless."

She shakes her head. "Good point."

We take my SUV to the station. Aside from the crew that's on duty, I'm the first to arrive for the ceremony. I lead Carly into my office, and she sits across from me. Wrangling the dirty thoughts in my head increases in difficulty the more time I spend with her.

Time speeds up shortly after our arrival, beginning with a knock on my office door. I look up to find Chief Bertoni filling the narrow space.

"Morning, Chief."

"Rhodes."

Carly rises to her feet. She introduces herself while it should be my place to do the same. In my mind I stumble over the correct words.

She extends her hand to him. "Hello, Chief Bertoni. Carly Reed. Pleasure to see you again."

"From York Memorial Emergency?"

"Yes, sir." Concern is twined through her response.

"Your work with the staff was admirable. It is my understanding they are willing to accept the counterproposal from the board."

Good for her. I wonder who Bertoni knows at the hospital who would be directly affected.

"Thank you. I haven't heard that yet. Is Janie Kuhn your daughter?"

This moment when Carly connects every dot makes me fall a little harder. While I'm aware she hated the politics of her staff's demands, she handled the added requirements with grace under pressure.

"Yes, she is."

"I'm happy to hear the staff may be willing to forego organizing a union."

"As am I." Bertoni turns his attention to me again. "The ceremony will be simple. The first officer will play the national anthem and then you will take the oath with the current Captain Rhodes, your mother, and your sister by your side"

I look pointedly at my—*my? Definitely*—beautiful girlfriend, and she nods nearly imperceptibly. "Carly will be with my family as well."

"Wonderful." I don't miss the underlying "about time" and "happy for you" in the chief's response.

Another person hovers near the door. He's short, but I know who it is. "Hello, Halston."

He weaves his way into my office to stand beside me as Bertoni leaves.

"Hi. Mom sent me to tell you we're in Bay One. Hi, Miss Carly." My nephew waves at her.

Carly smiles and waves back.

"Thanks. Please go back to your mom. We will be out soon."

"Got it." Halston skirts around the desk and disappears.

I move beside her and hold her hands in mine. An unmatched fit, if you ask me. "You okay with this?"

"Yes. Internally, I'm prepared for the questions but not sure I truly want to answer them."

"The reply you provided to Hagen and Lacey will work for almost everyone."

"Not Landry," she replies. "I gave him a piece of my mind for not sharing his girlfriend with me."

"We can talk to him together at Morgan's. Don't beat yourself up. It's only been a few months for us"

She acknowledges me and lifts her gaze to mine. "Congratulations, Alden. I'm proud of you."

No woman in years has said those words to me who wasn't related by blood. It's both heartbreaking and nice to hear at the same time. It was my choice to be closed off before now. I'm glad I took the leap with her. "Thank you." I kiss her and lead her into the bay with our hands linked. I greet my family. I don't miss the questions on their faces about Carly. I also know they won't press for information immediately. Her presence illustrates she's important to me. I appreciate that immensely.

The familiar tones of the nation's song echo in the large garage space. I gaze over at my family. My mother, sister, brother-in-law, and nephews are smiling widely. I'm sure the boys are happier about missing school than the actual event. I find myself staring at Carly, who is sitting beside Halston, rather than watching the actual color guard or Bertoni's opening remarks. I see potential. I see a future for us, and I'm excited to tell her.

Bertoni's words filter into my mind. "… exemplary service to the community. Ladies and gentleman, please rise."

The crowd stands. Bertoni and Uncle Stephon step to the side of the podium bearing the York Fire seal.

Bertoni continues while my uncle stands in front of me. We are perpendicular to the crowd.

"Ready for this?" the current captain asks.

"I've been working for this my entire career."

Uncle Stephon drops his head. "This house is in excellent hands."

His statement evokes mixed feelings for me. Those words should be coming from my father. However, I'm grateful he sees my potential too. "I will serve it well."

"I know. Your father would be beaming today."

The stab of grief washes over me, not only my father but for Asha and our little girl. I manage to acknowledge his sentiments without losing my composure.

Bertoni addresses me. "Please raise your right and state the oath."

I push down a sliver of doubt and state, "I, Alden M. Rhodes, do solemnly affirm that I will support the Constitution of the United States and the Constitution and laws of the State of Maine, and that I will faithfully and impartially discharge and perform the duties of Captain for the York Fire Department according to the best of my abilities, and agreeably to the rules and regulations of the Constitution and laws of the Commonwealth, so help me God."

Bertoni changes the pins on my collar while Uncle Stephon exchanges the patch on my arm.

"Ladies and gentlemen, I would like to introduce Captain Alden Rhodes," Uncle Stephon announces to the room.

Cheers and applause bounce off the concrete walls. I move behind the podium and share a few words about my appreciation for the house as well as the community. I'm sure my speech should've been longer, but the pomp and circumstance of the position isn't high on my list. I simply want to serve my community the best way I know how.

"Thank you." I end my speech and shake hands with the chief and my uncle before hugging my family. As I walk toward them, Carly falls in step with me. I twine my fingers with hers and draw her against me. I have no intention of letting her go. Claiming Carly as mine here and in front of these people is invigorating.

My mom speaks first, "Congratulations! Your father would be so proud of you continuing the Rhodes legacy at this house."

"Thank you."

I chat with the rest of my family and accept their well-wishes. The crew that was on duty has scattered throughout the house.

"I'll be back in a few to head over to the restaurant," I inform my mother.

"Of course," she replies.

The guys who aren't on duty are patiently waiting to chat with me. I take a step toward them without releasing Carly's hand.

Collings greets me first. "Congrats, Cap. I would like to request—"

"No." My answer is unequivocal but in a joking manner.

Foster laughs and adds, "Looking forward to your leadership, Rhodes. Any idea who is replacing you?"

I completely forgot about that requirement. "I have a list of candidates and will be interviewing over the next few shifts."

Foster replies, "Understood."

When I look to greet Landry who was at the end of the line, he isn't there anymore. Instead, he's with Mia beside him speaking with my mother. Before returning to my family, I turn my back to them and talk to Carly.

"Thank you for being here. I wanted to greet you first, but it didn't work out. I don't have appropriate words to express how much I appreciate your presence."

"You're welcome. I understand, truly."

I lean down and kiss her lips lightly. Our gaze holds for a minute of silence. While no words are spoken, the comfort and calm she provides is shouting loudly.

"Morgan's?" I ask.

"Sure." We turn and notice Landry, Mia, and my mother chatting it up.

"Does Landry talk to Mama Rhodes often?" she asks.

"No, not at all." It has been more frequent since…. *No. She wouldn't set me up.*

Carly adds, "That's interesting."

"What?" I ask but my mind is partially stuck on possibly being fixed up after all these years by my mother.

"I'm going to surmise Mia is Landry's girlfriend by their proximity and body language. That is who we were going to pair up."

"Wow. Your dating sense is unmatched."

She shrugs. "I guess so. Still wish he trusted me with the information."

As we approach the group, I hear my mother say, "… it worked out well for them. Thank you."

Curious. What would my mother be thanking Landry for?

Landry and Mia leave before Carly can greet him. I would prefer him to spill the beans and let me off the hook for already knowing.

We exit the station and walk to my SUV. I notice my family is pulling out of the lot. When we arrive, Landry pulls into the spot beside us.

Rather than wait for me to open her door, Carly hops out.

"Hey, bro."

"Hey. I didn't want to disturb you during the ceremony. I bet you're glad I sent Rhodes in my place for the softball game planning."

I overhear his words, but they aren't news to me. He did ask me to replace him, and it was definitely a stellar decision on my part to agree.

Mia exits the car and moves beside Landry. "Hi, I'm Mia. It's nice to finally meet you."

"You as well."

"I mean we filled out that form months ago."

Landry gives a pointed look at Mia, and Carly turns toward me.

Damn it!

"You knew and didn't share?" Carly asks me.

"Those forms are confidential. It wasn't my place." I defend my choice. She would do the same in my position. I'm sure of it.

"I see. Please excuse me." Carly, with slumped shoulders and a sigh, walks away from me on one of the biggest days of my life in anger. On one hand, I want to chase after her. I can't. This reception is for me. Part of me doesn't care, but I will do the right thing anyway.

I look to Landry. "Fix this. I didn't do anything wrong here. Your choice is messing with my relationship. Please do it now."

"I'm sorry," Mia mutters. "I didn't know."

Landry replies, "This is my fault. I'll meet you inside." He kisses Mia's cheek and follows his sister.

Slowly, I make my way into the building. I would prefer to smooth this over myself, but it won't work. Landry must do this himself. If this reception wasn't for me, I would go home immediately.

Morgan's is a high-end restaurant owned and operated by August Morgan. They have a dining room as well as a few private spaces that can be rented out. The building overlooks the harbor and has spectacular views.

I enter the Caroline room… alone. I want to throttle Landry for dragging his feet about Mia. My sole reason is Carly. I understand completely where he is coming from. Hell, we were keeping things private as well. I don't think that's the issue. Her anger is because I knew Mia's identity and didn't share with my girlfriend.

Carly will see the reason, and she'll understand. She would never divulge information from work. Nor will I. Are the levels of confidentiality the same? Not really but the underlying principle is.

The room is filled with people milling about to celebrate me. I'm no longer in the mood.

"Alden." My mom's voice pulls me out of my thoughts.

"Yeah."

Gladys Rhodes is a strong woman. She also knows when something is off with her children. "Are you okay?"

"Not really." I glance toward the marina and see Landry and Carly on the deck. I wouldn't call the conversation a heated exchange, but it's clear she's mad at him. Me too probably.

"She's wonderful, Alden." I'm sure her opinion is informed by previous book club meetings and charity events as well as her presence this afternoon.

She is. Part of me wishes I came out of my shell earlier. That decision would've given me more time with her. "I may have messed up our budding relationship by doing my job. It's a long story that is still unfolding as we speak, but... yes, Carly is amazing."

"Your smile hasn't reached your eyes in years. It does with her beside you or when you're staring at her."

I hadn't realized that, but thinking about it, she's right. "Thanks, Mom."

She sets her hand on my forearm. "Don't give up. You deserve to have a person in your life again. Nothing about... relationships is easy."

"I know." I check on Carly again and see her still arguing with Landry. The urge to intrude is strong, but I fight it and remain in the dining room.

Stalking from afar.

CHAPTER SEVENTEEN

CARLY

Anger is coursing through me as I stomp my way through the building to the rear deck overlooking the water. Who I'm most angry with is the biggest question on my mind.

My brother—for stupid reasons—didn't share his relationship with Mia before today. The truth is they have been dating for nearly eight months at this point. He didn't trust me. That stings more than I care to admit. Sure, I'm part of the Matchmaker's Book Club, but we are good at selecting our couples. While I didn't agree to take him off the list, I did agree to push off his coupling. We were right about the best woman for him. The group voted to pair him with Mia.

It doesn't upset me that they got together on their own. Good for them. It would've been easier for me if I knew and deleted him as an honoree because he was happily in a relationship. Instead, he tried to bribe me with lunch and a ubiquitous promise to meet the woman later. A delicious sandwich, but that isn't important.

It was impossible to miss the chemistry between Landry and Mia today. They seem to be doing well. It didn't cross my mind until Mia shared about the relationship form in the parking lot that Alden could've have known her identity.

Alden. My sexy as hell boyfriend has been put in the middle of this. It wasn't his fault. He was doing the—

"Carly!"

I shake my head and turn away from my brother's sharp tone. His footfalls are heavy on the wooden planks.

Landry circles me, forcing me to look at him despite my desire to turn away like the petulant little sister I am. "Don't blame Rhodes. This is all on me. Your group isn't a secret in this town anymore. I wanted to find a woman on my own. I also needed to be sure my relationship was going somewhere before I told you."

"Bullshit. After everything our parents put us through… the fights and numerous partners, I thought we were a team against bad relationship choices. If you were sure about the existence of the matchmakers, you should have opted out. You didn't trust me. There probably isn't a group anymore so mission accomplished."

Landry frowns. "That wasn't my goal."

"Doesn't matter. It's the result."

My brother huffs and adds, "I wanted to date in private like you."

I shake my head. "It isn't the same, and you know it."

"It's not?"

"No. You purposely shut me out of your dating life. I get it. The group makes things dicey and intrusive. You could've told me your concerns about being fixed up."

Landry drags his hand down his face. "I tried. Maybe too late, but... Rhodes didn't do anything wrong."

I know, and the hollow in my stomach for walking away is gnawing at my heart.

"Sure, he was aware about me and Mia because of the HR form. He couldn't share the information with you."

"Except we talked about you and your unnamed girlfriend, and he still didn't share with me."

Landry shakes his head. "You should be more impressed with his integrity. Rhodes protected my privacy. No man you dated before has ever made you as happy as him. Don't ruin what seems to be a promising relationship with Rhodes because I didn't tell you about Mia sooner."

Oh hell. "Damn it, Landry."

"I'm sorry. I didn't realize sharing about Mia would have the same effect as requesting removal."

My big brother is precisely right. Of course, Alden should have protected the information. He was required to. My beef is with Landry, not... Ugh! "Can you ask him to join me out here?" I realize that isn't ideal, as the party is for him, but....

"Yeah."

"Thanks."

Landry turns on his heel and starts to walk away. Turning back, he adds, "I meant what I said. If you're happy and care about Rhodes, don't give up so easily."

I acknowledge his words and survey the marina again. It's peaceful and serene. The fact Landry can see my feelings fosters hope for me... and Alden. Everything is nearly perfect with Alden. Only nearly because we still have a few big things to discuss.

Despite his stature, I don't hear Alden approach. I've been drawn to him for years. Now, I feel him when he's nearby. "Hi." I turn and extend my hand to him.

He takes it and replies in kind.

The heat from his touch streaks up my arm. "I'm sorry. I was pissed at my brother and reacted poorly."

Alden eliminates the space between us and cups my face with his free hand. "I understand. I considered sharing, but I couldn't violate their trust. I would expect the same from any member of my house."

"As you should."

He leans closer and kisses me without regard for his guests inside the venue, who can probably see us. I'm not mad about it. He makes me feel lighter and calmer. Plus, the more people who know, the sooner the questions will settle down.

Adding some space, I say, "I hope I didn't ruin the reception for you."

Alden gifts me with a sly smile and a wink. "I would prefer to stay out here with you. Big groups of people, especially gathered in my honor, aren't an ideal way to spend my time."

"Got it. No large events."

"Unfortunately, I need to go back inside. Will you come with me?"

As long as you'll have me. I nod and kiss him lightly. With our fingers twined, we return to the reception. Alden spends the next hour shaking hands and chatting about the changes he's considering at the firehouse.

Landry and Mia have been talking with Gladys in the corner of the room. Their coziness makes me think something is up between them. Observing my brother in a committed relationship is new for me as well. I know Mia as a member of his house, and I've interacted with her maybe six times before today. She's younger than me, but the age gap doesn't appear to be an issue.

"Carly." Alden calls me. A beautiful smile is on his chiseled face. His mocha skin is smooth and flawless.

I gaze up at him and match his grin. "Yes?"

"Are you ready to leave?"

I wrinkle my nose. "Whenever you are. It is your party, after all."

"Funny."

We cross the room and stop near Gladys.

"We're going to head home. Thank you for being here today. I'm sure it was difficult for you."

Gladys glances lovingly at her only son and replies, "I appreciate you, Alden. Everything is as it should be. I'll see you both at the next family dinner."

I want to beg off because it's foreign to me that people have calm meals on a regular basis with their family members. However, being with him means learning to be comfortable with the new things. "Can't wait."

We walk to his SUV, and he opens my door.

"What do we feel like doing tomorrow?" He's actually asking me, and I ponder for a few moments while Alden turns toward his home.

"Are you up for a local date?"

He tilts his head in interest. "Everyone knows about us now. What do you have in mind?"

I laugh. "I'm suggesting strolling in the village, stopping at the beach, and kicking your ass in bowling at the arcade. Perhaps not in that order. Then we should probably grab ice cream."

"You're on. I'll pick you up at nine?"

He parks in his driveway and hurries around the hood of his vehicle. He smirks at me as he walks. If being with Alden is like the last few weeks, I could remain happy. True, we disagreed today. No, I overreacted. Either way, we talked and handled it like adults with good communication. While my dating history is spotty, both of my exes failed mightily in that area. Alden is a grown man and I'm grateful how we handled the issue.

With a flourish, he offers me his arm and escorts me to my driver door. "Thank you for coming today." Alden slides his hands around my waist and draws me close.

I gaze up at him. The look on his face is nothing short of admiration. I can only hope mine mirrors his. "I wouldn't have missed it. Your promotion is a big deal. I'm crazy proud of you. That beats my desire to keep our relationship private, hands down."

He eliminates the space between us and kisses me until the stars above us have taken up residence in my eyes. No man ever made me feel like he does.

Preventing myself from falling hard and deeply will be nearly impossible. In my mind, we only have one more huge issue to discuss. It's big for most relationships.

I pull away and say, "Good night, Alden."

"Sleep well, sweetheart. You're going to need the energy to beat me."

With a wink, I add, "Doubtful."

"Please text me when you get home." Alden opens my car door.

"I will."

He waits on the concrete until I pull away. Upon arrival, I text him.

Me: I'm home. xoxo.

Alden M. Rhodes: Rest up. I'll be there in the morning.

Me: See you then.

Sunlight streams through my window. *I'm late.* I sit up quickly and glance at the clock. When my eyes focus, I see it's only 7:30. I get ready for my day with Alden. Surprisingly, I can be with him, and he doesn't get on my nerves. It's a good sign for our future. Both of my previous long-term boyfriends didn't have the same effect.

I prepare a coffee for Alden and a tea for me and wait for him on the front porch. Most mornings, especially in the summer months, I rise early enough to enjoy the sunshine before work.

A smile grows on my face when he pulls to a stop behind my car. "Hi, beautiful," he states as he walks in my direction.

"Morning."

"You excited?" he asks while bounding up the wooden stairs.

"Yes, but I drink my tea out here in the warmer months."

"Sounds nice."

"Feel free to join me anytime. In fact," I reach beside me and extend his coffee to him, "take a seat."

Alden grabs the travel mug, kisses me lightly, and then joins me. After a healthy sip or two and a few solid minutes of quiet, he says, "This is a nice way to start the day."

"After swimming?"

"Yeah."

We enjoy the birds chirping and the other nature sounds for a while.

"Ready?"

"Are you?" he asks.

"I always am."

We laugh and drive to the village. When I was young, walking the street and shopping seemed like an arduous task. I would guess the round trip and surrounding shops down a perpendicular road is perhaps a mile at most.

Our first stop is The Perk for refills of our drinks. We stroll along the cobblestone road and duck into one of the stores. They have seasonal tees along the walls along with hoodies emblazoned with the town name or Maine. As a child, I was mesmerized by how the staff could add any design to a plain shirt so quickly.

We browse in the shops along the street. When we near our starting point, an older gentlemen flags Alden down.

"Good morning. I'm sorry to bother you."

Alden replies, "No trouble at all."

"I'm one of the owners of the restaurant." We're standing in front of the building where the car crashed through the window. There is a board in place of the glass and the paint is in the midst of being repaired. "Thank you for your work that day. We will be able to reopen this season because you supported the building properly."

"You're welcome, sir." They shook hands, and we enter the shop around the corner. "Sorry about that," he says near the shell of my ear.

"No worries," I manage. It seems to me, at least with him, physical closeness is exceptional. It may even be my love language, while his is acts of service.

Near eleven, we cross the street and enter the bowling alley next door to Fun-O-Rama, which houses an arcade alongside the beach.

"What size?" the attendant asks.

We change our shoes and set up the scoreboard.

"What do I get if I win?" he asks with a glint of mischief in his eye.

I may have picked the wrong activity to assure a victory on my part. "Bragging rights?"

"Deal."

It's clear in the first five frames Alden can bowl, and well.

"Did you leave out you're a ringer?" He has a score of 150 to my measly 45.

He gifts me with a gorgeous smile that showcases his dimples, which only adds to his charm. "Not a ringer. My dad and uncle were avid bowlers. I may have picked up a few things."

"I see." I take my lumps, and he beats me handily for the three games we play.

We laugh and return our rental shoes. With our hands threaded together, we wander along the concrete path. About halfway, I pause. "Do you want to turn back?" I'm surprised he said yes to a date in the village. Walking by the location of Asha's accident isn't necessary.

Alden kisses my temple and murmurs, "I'm okay. I couldn't avoid the area forever. Slowly, over the years, I made peace with this stretch of beach being the last place she was alive."

I turn my head and gaze up at him. I love how tall he is. His facial expression matches his words. The shoreline is filled with beachgoers having a great time. After walking three lengths of Short Sands, we take a seat on one of the green wooden benches.

"How does pizza and a movie sound?" he asks.

I'm distracted by his fingertips sliding casually along the curve of my neck. He makes my heart rate spike with the simplest touch. I clear my throat. "Perfect."

We make our way back to my house and order delivery. I hand him the remotes. "I have nearly every possible subscription available, despite a lack of time to watch to make it worthwhile."

"Any restrictions?" he asks.

"No horror. I avoid anime as well."

He laughs heartily and scrolls through the options. Alden chooses *Captain America: Brave New World.*

We snuggle up on the couch, and after our pizza arrives, we start the film. After we inhale every single slice of veggie pizza, I worm my way between the back cushion of the couch and Alden. You would think sleeping against him wouldn't be comfy. Surprisingly, it is. So much so, we are awakened by his alarm for work at five the next morning. The television is still on, and our dinner plates and glasses are on the coffee table.

Alden hops to his feet quickly. "I need to go. My uniform is at home. What are your plans today?"

"Some last-minute checks for the game and then reading. Have a quiet shift."

"Dinner on Wednesday?"

"If you're cooking, I'm there."

He laughs and kisses me deeply. Too long based on the fact he needs to leave immediately. He shouldn't be late on his first official day as Captain. I'll happily accept each kiss he wants to give me. "I'll call you later." He pulls away and disappears out my front door.

I love waking up with him. The notion hits me hard. I never wanted that before, not even with Kenneth, who asked me to marry him. Thankfully, I listened to my gut and took time before answering. Then again, agreeing to be with him forever would've forced him to come clean about the fact he already had a wife.

Alden is in a class by himself, and I'm excited for us.

CHAPTER EIGHTEEN

ALDEN

My shift at the station is over. Overall, it was peaceful with no major calls. Instead of heading straight home, I decide to surprise Carly.

She literally hops off her front steps and runs to the driveway to greet me.

"Morning," I state while lifting her off the ground. Her petite stature is one of my favorite things about her.

She peppers my mouth with kisses. "I don't hate this surprise. In fact, I kind of love it."

When we break for air, I ask, "Do you hate them normally?"

She shrugs. "Until now, the others were failures. I guess successful ones are fine with me."

"Understood. How much time do we have?"

She twists her wrist, and then frowns.

"Not much, huh?"

With a pouty look on her face and her lower lip pushed out, she answers, "No."

I restrain myself from pulling that lip between my teeth and focus on my reason for showing up this morning. "I realize it seems a tad old-fashioned at this point but…. Will you be my date to the First In, Last Out Ball?"

"Yes, I would love to." She kisses me deeply.

I don't care that we're standing in her driveway. Now that our family and friends know about us, I'm forgoing the safeguards I would otherwise employ.

Too soon, she adds space between us. "I need to go to work. Are we still on for dinner?"

"Absolutely." I lower her to the gravel.

"Go, before I'm tempted to call in."

I raise an eyebrow, loving the idea of spending the entire day with her again. Truly, her company is unmatched. "Would that be so bad?"

"Hanging out with you? Not at all. In fact, it sounds wonderful. However, I can't call in after taking a day off without a good reason. Not that you—" She buries her head into my chest.

"I'll meet you here for dinner." I kiss her forehead and retreat to my SUV. I don't want her to be late because of me. When I arrive home, I change and dive right into the cool water.

Halfway through my first lap, I recall Asha believed in me from the moment we met. The kicker is Carly does as well. Showing up at the ceremony last week couldn't have been easy. For me... for us, she did exactly that. My next thought is my daughter. Alicia would be president of her class. A few laps later, I recall the anniversary of Asha's death is tomorrow. I'll never forget, but progress in my grief means the date doesn't linger in the back of my mind every waking minute. Nor is there a countdown like for the first one. I swim another mile before internally stating a positive aspect of my day. I fulfilled my goal to have a date for the ball.

My action item is to own my feelings for Carly, even if I don't share them verbally. I finish 1000 meters and climb out of the pool.

I towel off, grab some breakfast, and walk to my workshop. I'm more than halfway done with Carly's gift. The wood pieces are cut and sanded. I need to stain, seal, and assemble the chairs. If I have time, I'll build a small table as well. I didn't have a specific occasion in mind though.

I set up the painting booth in the shop and apply the first coat. I return to the kitchen for a water. A little bit later, I add a second coat. As I wrap up and take a break, my phone rings.

"Hey, Raf. How's it going?"

"Pretty good. Thanks. Mauro and I are considering adopting a baby. Congrats on the promotion." I don't need to remind him of the importance of tomorrow.

"Much appreciated. That's amazing. You've always dreamed of being a father. Good for you."

"It took me some time to get over the fact it wouldn't be with Elio. You?"

"Shockingly good. Carly and I attended an event together. Despite me wanting to keep her to myself a little longer, it went well." I invited Rafael, but he couldn't switch his schedule so quickly. Raf doesn't need to know about the issue with Landry and Mia.

"I need to meet this woman who can make you smile. I can hear it through the phone."

I laugh. "I'll see what I can do. A cookout soon? My next weekend evening off is in a few weeks."

"Sounds perfect. I'm available tomorrow at ten like always."

"Thank you." One of the suggestions in our grief group was to allow time for calls but don't force them. Raf and I designated the 10 a.m. hour for ours. If we need to talk about Asha, Alicia, or Elio, we simply have to pick up the phone. Could we call at other times? Of course, but that hour is always available for both of us, no questions asked. On one occasion, we simply sat on an open phone line without saying a word. Other times Raf and I shared stories about our lost loves. One conversation included talk about Alicia and his plan to have a child via surrogate with Elio.

The idea of having a family with Carly doesn't scare me. As I mentioned to her, I would love to have the opportunity to be a dad. Noting the hour, I sweep up the shop and clean up for dinner. It's a tad early, but I need to go to the grocery store and the florist.

Shortly after I arrive and move the bags to the porch, Carly pulls into her parking spot. I jump to the bottom of the stairs and greet her with a kiss. It's as if I can't get enough of her. She brings light into my days like Asha but different. Carly is being herself, while Asha was fulfilling the requirements her parents forced on her. As the oldest and only daughter, she was required to be above reproach, excel in school, and still be able to network an entire room of her father's business associates. A few minutes later, I add space. "Hi."

"Hi, yourself." She laughs softly, kisses me lightly once more, and enters the house. "How was your day?"

"Good. Productive with my latest project in the shop, and I spoke with Rafael. He would like to meet you."

Carly turns in my direction. "Same for me. Maybe we can have a get-together. Willa and Scarlett are dying to hang out as couples as well."

"Works for me. My next Saturday off?"

"Perfect. Can I help you with dinner?"

I frown at her. "No thank you. I would prefer these ingredients remain edible."

She feigns anger. "Can I at least make the salad? I can manage that no problem."

"Have at it."

A little while later, we sit and enjoy dinner, complete with salad and flank steak with mashed potatoes and asparagus. The rest of the evening, we talk until she's ready to go to sleep. I don't want my time with her to end. I haven't since our first meeting for the softball game. For someone with my history, that's a huge deal, especially considering the significance of tomorrow. Despite my desire to wake up with Carly, I return home for the night.

The next morning, I jump into the pool. My thoughts begin with my wife and daughter. The passing years have lessened the weight of the loss, but I still carry it daily. My thoughts don't follow their normal pattern today. I've come to accept that this day, the one where I lost them, changes each time the calendar reaches late June. When my arms feel like noodles, I climb the stairs and take a shower.

I gulp down a cup of coffee, grab the flowers from the fridge, and drive to see my girls. Visiting was more frequent in the early days. Now, I purposefully stand with them at least three times a year: on Asha's birthday, our wedding anniversary, and the date I lost them. Although, I missed our wedding anniversary this year because I was working a long call. I try not to beat myself up about it.

When I park at the cemetery, I notice a woman beside their gravestone. Those curves haunt my heart and soul daily. What is Carly doing here? How does she know where my family is buried? The longer I stand at the edge of the grass, the more questions pop into my head.

Rather than give her space, I slowly approach.

Carly doesn't hear me. Either I've improved my stealth skills, or she's deep in thought. Wordlessly, I stop beside her.

"Alden, I...." She stops her thought short as if she isn't allowed to be here. That begs the question, why is she here.

I notice two single white roses atop their gravestone. Identical flowers were left beginning on the first anniversary and always before I arrived. Now the flowers make sense. She was visiting before work. "It was you? All these years?"

"Yes." Carly turns and meets my gaze fully.

I hold back the tears forming in my eyes. "Why?" My voice cracks as the question passes through my lips.

"Asha and—" Her eyes close briefly then refocus on me.

"Alicia. I call her Alicia," I offer.

"They were the first patients I lost in my career. I honor them and use their memory as a reminder to advocate hard for my patients every single day."

I take her hand and lift it to my lips, kissing the back. "I don't have appropriate words in this moment for my gratitude and appreciation of you." I could probably come up with three small but mighty words. Here is not the right time nor place to share them aloud, even if they are accurate and true.

"Thank you. Neither do I for you." She rises on her toes and kisses my cheek. "I need to go to work." Carly squeezes my hand, releases it, and walks in the opposite direction to her car. I don't miss her swipe away a tear despite staring at her from behind. Her presence was comforting.

I watch until she pulls away before returning my attention to my wife and daughter's grave. Standing here feels different this year. My thoughts are lighter and less sad. I remember the good times I had with Asha from our pizza date to the first look at our wedding. Those are pleasant. Each happy memory of Alicia is fictional. I accepted she was born sleeping long ago. Moving forward with Carly means making space, and understanding being with her and happy isn't a violation of my vows. I will never forget the first ladies of my life, but it's time for me to own my feelings for Carly and any daughters we may have in the future.

CHAPTER NINETEEN

CARLY

It's finally here. I feel like I've been planning this day forever. I'm not even angry I had to get up at the crack of dawn on a weekend. Armed with a cup of tea, breakfast, and my glove, I head to the fields.

The rec plex allows us to hold two games at once. There are eight teams for the single elimination tournament. We will crown a new champion at the end of the day. Ideally, the trophy will reside at the hospital this year. While we didn't practice much at all, I have a little bit of hope.

"Morning, gorgeous."

I spin and find Alden stalking toward me. I set down my stuff and run toward him. Somehow I've missed him since I saw him last. Without a second thought, I leap into his arms. I have no doubt he'll catch me. He's meeting me here because he just got off work. Hopefully, the lack of sleep for him and his teammates will boost me and mine to victory.

It's been a few days since the anniversary of losing his wife and daughter. We talked at length over dinner about keeping their memories alive while moving forward together. We're in a good place.

"Hi to you too."

Someone clears their throat. "No consorting with the enemy, Rhodes."

I laugh at Landry's words without looking at him.

Mia adds, "Leave them alone. They're so sweet together."

I turn and reply, "Thank you." I'm happy for them. Their relationship seems solid.

"Most welcome. How can we help?"

Alden sets me on my feet and throws his arm over my shoulder. "I have you and my brother manning the registration table since your game isn't until ten. Hagen separated the shirts by team and added field information. You need to collect the donations as well."

"No problem," she answers.

"I bet you're glad I didn't show up for the planning meeting," Landry states, looking squarely at me.

I lift my eyes up to Alden and back to my brother. "I'm not mad about it."

Landry adds, "I'm sure Mama Rhodes is happy too."

Curious phrasing, but I don't address his statement. "Get movin'. Teams are starting to arrive."

"Where did you assign me?" Alden leans close to my ear and whispers.

I can't contain the shiver he causes. "You know better than to do that in public."

He winks at me. "Do I, or is it on purpose?"

"You are with me until game time. Please prepare yourself and your team to lose."

"You still got it, Reed?" He questions my skill set.

"Can I still pitch? Yes, nearly as well as in high school. Plus, I know how to strike out at least half of your batting order."

His eyes widen, but he says nothing else.

Maybe half was an exaggeration, but psyching out my opponent is worth it.

"Let's check on Penn and get this thing started."

We wander to the far side of the field near the medical area with our hands linked and a spring in our step.

"Hey, Carly. Alden," Penn greets us. He agreed to run the medical tent to avoid playing. I appreciate the sacrifice. Otherwise, I would've been caring for the injured instead of pitching.

"All set?" I ask.

"Yup. The turnout seems to be better than last year. Good for you," Penn replies.

"Thank you."

"I forgot to inquire…. Tatum and Zara want to take photos if that is okay with you."

"Absolutely. That would be awesome."

Penn smiles. "I'll let them know. See you later."

I glance at my watch. "Shoot. We gotta hurry!" A light jog later, I stop between the two fields and climb to the top of the bleachers.

"Good morning, and welcome to this year's charity softball event. A champion will be crowned and earn the right to house the trophy until next year. May the odds be ever in your favor. Play ball!"

I take in a few innings of each game that starts before mine. The "Team of Dads" are being crushed by the YPD team. On the other field, the EMTs are tied with the York Beach High softball team.

Alden has been quietly beside me as I traipse around checking on everything. "This is great, sweetheart."

"Thank you. I was able to delegate most of the planning,"

He shakes his head. "Don't downplay your efforts. It took work. I saw only some of it."

I lean forward and kiss him. I'm so lost in the swirling emotions, I forget where we are. It happens every single time.

Whistles begin from our left.

"Woohoo!"

Alden adds a sliver of space. "That's Essie and probably my mother."

I nod and turn toward the noise.

Essie, her sons, and Gladys approach the bottom of the bleachers.

"Good morning! It's a great day for a game or two."

She's right. Despite it being late June, the temperature isn't oppressively hot or humid today. He greets his nephews with their signature handshake and hugs his mom and sister. I fist-bump the boys and follow suit with hugs for Essie and Gladys.

"Are you staying for my game?" Alden asks them.

Halston replies, "Yes. We're here to see Miss Carly pitch too."

Inwardly, I laugh. The YFD and York Memorial team are facing off in thirty minutes. The matchups were selected randomly by picking numbers. "Thanks, Halston."

"Uncle Alden was talking about you. He said you were like really, really good in high school."

I shrug. "I can hold my own."

Alden and I excuse ourselves to warm up alongside the field.

"What do I get if I win?" I ask him.

"A trophy and bragging rights, I guess."

I raise my shoulder in tacit acceptance. "Are we allowed to kiss before the game?"

"Allowed, I don't care. It's happening either way." He draws me into his arms and kisses me breathless.

"No making out with the opposing pitcher, Cap."

Alden turns to see who is catcalling us. "Not on the mound yet, Foster."

The teams present their lineups, and we take the field. I haven't pitched a game in about a year. My recreational league disbanded. I'm okay with it. I would prefer to spend my free time with Alden anyway. I glance over at him in the dugout and then quickly look away. *No distractions. Not even a hot-as-hell, muscular man you call your boyfriend.* Three up, three down. *Let's go, Reed.*

With ease, I dispatch the first and second batters on four pitches. Next up is Landry.

I'm calm and collected on the mound with my brother at the plate. I throw a fastball off the outside of the plate, and he swings wildly.

I glance at the bleachers and see Alden's family cheering us both on. It feels foreign but I kind of love it, Landry's words from earlier echo in my head.

Holy crap! Who would set us up? The girls in book club agreed to allow me to wait. There isn't anyone else. I push the thought away until after I strike out the side.

Two pitches later, I throw a curve on the inside corner, and Landry skulks back to the dugout.

The next four innings play out in similar fashion. The only activity is a triple by Dr. Jonah Mitchell in the bottom of the fifth. Unfortunately, he gets stranded on base.

When we reach the seventh and last inning of the game, I sit down the side with a little fielding help. I throw out Foster. Alden is grounded to short, and Landry lofts a fly ball to shallow left field. I literally hop up and down on the mound before shaking hands with our opponents.

Alden is at the end of the line. "Good game, sweetheart."

I smile and ask, "Can you stay, or do you need sleep?"

He leans closer, holding up the high fives. "No place I would rather be than with you."

While York Memorial crushed YFD, Park and Rec play a formidable opponent with the York High Baseball team. I know how difficult it is to switch between a softball and a baseball, since I started out playing with the boys. Either way, the two York High teams will face off in round two.

I have about thirty minutes to rest before game two against YPD. I would like to bounce them out to make sure they don't hold onto the trophy for two years in a row. At the same time, the high school teams will play as well. We may need to pool our resources to defeat the younger and faster teens so the trophy remains with one of the first responder teams. Is that against the rules? Most definitely. Do I want the high school to house the trophy until next year? Absolutely not.

With Alden sitting with his mom and sister in the stands for this game, I walk out to the rubber and take a deep breath. I stare at him for longer than necessary. When I pan out and see a happy family, a stab of longing hits me. I never had that. I want it... for me and hopefully the children we will have…. *Whoa!*

Normally, I would freak out about my desire to provide a better life for my future children than my childhood was for me. Now that I see it's possible, I'm going to own my wants and chase after them. I ignore the niggling conversation Alden and I still need to have, but otherwise, I'm ready. Willingly I'll accept cheers, gifts, and meals from Alden's family because it's part of being with him. Internally, at least initially, I will feel prickly and scared. Over time, I will absorb the gestures and hold onto them for my children.

"Play ball!" the umpire shouts from behind home plate.

Centering myself on the rubber, I throw a perfect strike. The applause from the Rhodes family is heartwarming. This is what a cohesive group feels like. They're here, present, and offering support, even though Alden isn't on the field. I'm terrified but excited to accept the same.

"Yay! Miss Carly!" I believe that is Henry's voice.

I nod in his direction to indicate I heard them and then retire the side. This game is a bit harder than the last one. While my pitches are equally on point, the YPD team is much better at getting around on the ball. We're at the end of six innings. The game is knotted at one run each. In the middle of the seventh with the same score, thunder rumbles in the distance. Before the players clear the field, rain starts to fall heavily.

The umpires stop the two games in progress. I watch the radar loop. I'm not optimistic about finishing this game, nor playing the final. Nearly an hour later, after speaking with the officiating crew, we decide to postpone play for the day. I thank the participants and indicate a continuation will be planned if time and facilities allow. As I talk, I look throughout the crowd for Landry and Mia. Perhaps they left after the YFD loss in game one. Interestingly, his absence bothers me today. Without the Rhodes family sticking around, I wouldn't have noticed in the past.

Foster of the YFD shouts, "What about the trophy?"

The remaining crowd grumbles, and potential solutions are thrown around from the YPD to headquarters to me personally holding onto the golden cup.

I raise my hand, and the crowd quiets. "We don't have precedent for this situation. As the chairperson, as much as it pains me as I could feel victory was forthcoming, the YPD shall retain possession until we complete this tourney or the next charity game when it will be on the line, whichever comes first."

Members of the police department cheer, and others grouse, but this decision is the correct choice. The group disburses, and I join the Rhodes family where the registration tent once stood.

Alden takes off his jacket and throws it over my shoulders, even though he'll end up soaked as well.

"Thank you."

"Of course. Are you up for dinner with my family later?" He already knows I won't say no or he wouldn't ask here and now.

"Definitely, but a long, scalding shower is required first."

Gladys and Essie laugh and agree.

"We'll see you by six," Gladys states, and the group rushes away to their cars.

A pang of jealousy hits me. Alden had his family his entire life in good times and bad. I remind myself that dating him means gaining his family. Reconciling my past with wanting his mother and sister's attention, affection, and more importantly, accepting their support is harder than I anticipated.

"Carly?"

"Hmmm." I look over at him. The heavy rain molds his shirt to the planes of his chest and sculpted abs. My carnal desire to jump his bones runs as deep as the lowest point on earth. Talk to him first, I remind myself. He deserves the chance to walk away if my choice is too much for him. I would hate that with a fire of a thousand suns. Yet I feel as if the decision to stay or go should be his.

"Want to share the thoughts pinging in your head?"

"Yes, just not right this minute. I can meet you at your mom's if you want to go ahead or go home and get dry clothes."

He draws me against his solid frame, and I fight the urge to sigh. I was attracted to this man many years ago when he was a teenager. I didn't realize it then, but I'm drawn to him on a level I still don't understand in the present.

"Nope. I'm coming with you. I have clothes in my SUV. Then we can drive to dinner together. After a delicious meal, I could bring you home and maybe, just maybe, secure an amazing goodnight kiss."

I giggle and shake my head as we walk to the parking lot. He follows me to my house. I have plenty of time to get ready but feel gross covered in dirt from the field and then soaked by the rain.

"Do you want to take a shower?" I ask as soon as we're inside.

"I would appreciate that. You can go first though."

A soft laugh bubbles up. "I have two bathrooms. Come on." I extend my hand to him and lead him down the hall. With fresh towels from the linen closet, I leave him and escape to my en suite off the master.

I shower faster than normal. More because I'm nervous despite having met his family already but less about not having enough time. I towel off and throw on a gauzy sundress with bows at the shoulders. It's a tad outside my normal style, but it's comfortable. Before I put on makeup, I pad to the kitchen again.

When I exit the hallway, my mouth goes dry. Alden is standing near the island with only a towel wrapped at his waist.

Holy hell! He's hot as.... I refrain from fanning myself by the slimmest of margins.

He doesn't address my staring. Alden simply grabs his bag, kisses the tip of my nose, and disappears down the hall.

I grab a water and attempt to quench my thirst both literally and figuratively. As I'm refilling the glass, he returns fully dressed in a YFD shirt and athletic shorts.

"Am I overdressed for dinner?"

"You look beautiful. Not at all. This is what I have handy."

"Okay."

Rather than give me more grace to put off this conversation, he asks, "What were you thinking about at the field? You've had enough space to stew."

"Your family and then sex."

His eyes widen, and he chokes out, "What?"

My skin is likely beet red. It certainly feels blazing hot. "Yes, I said sex."

"With my mother and sister in close proximity?" His question is incredulous. He turns to face me but doesn't move.

"Not like that. It was about the support from your family. I never had that, and I was crazy jealous when they showed up for you. But then… they stayed when you weren't playing anymore for…."

"You," he supplies.

"Yeah. I didn't know what to do with it. The gesture made me happy but uncertain as well. I'm scared to want the support in the future. I'm sure it doesn't make any sense to you because you've always had people in your corner."

He smiles and replies, "My family is fantastic. They see the shift in me because of you. Mom and Essie won't be intrusive. Involved is more accurate."

"It's going to take some getting used to for me."

He nods and adds, "Completely understandable." Alden drapes his shirt on the stool and stalks toward me. A hairsbreadth of space is between me and his bare chest.

Holy hell.

"Sex?"

I rest my palm flat on him. The warmth from his skin sends prickles up my arm. His heart beats rapidly beneath my fingers. "The way your shirt was clinging to you made me want to… tear your clothes off."

"But…."

Exhaling slowly and deeply, I mumble, "My experience is limited and unpleasant."

Alden's body stiffens at the second descriptor. "Someone hurt you," he states in a hushed voice.

A shiver hurries down my spine. "Yes."

He lifts me into his arms. With a few long strides, Alden settles into the armchair with me in his lap.

For a few minutes, I absorb the comfort he's offering. "My past is a large part of the reason we've been moving slowly."

He shakes his head. "The pace isn't completely on you. I have reasons to be purposeful and cautious as well."

My eyes close briefly, and I calm my heart rate as best I can. "Five years ago, I learned my boyfriend Kenneth, who was a non-local doctor at York Memorial, had a wife and child in another state. He was here to learn under the head of cardiothoracic surgery for three years. We started dating within two months of his arrival. After an utterly horrible shift, I drove to his place instead of mine. The fact I had never been there before didn't cross my mind. Nothing about him made me suspect he was a liar and adulterer. No line where a ring should've been or any slip-ups about a child." I drop my head. "All that is to say, his wife answered the door and called me vile things from whore to trollop to homewrecker. As soon as I could, I booked a solo trip to the Bahamas."

My entire body shakes nearly uncontrollably the closer I get to sharing my assault with Alden. Only my girls know because they were there to pick up the pieces and put me back together. Not quite like Humpty Dumpty but close.

"The details don't matter to me, but you feel like you need to share, right?" Alden murmurs against my temple.

"I do. He stole from me. You deserve the option to walk away."

Anger vibrates through him. "Why would you think that?"

I fail to suppress the tears pooling at the corner of my eyes. "I made some choices you might not be able to live with."

His jaw clenches. "The assault was not your fault. Full stop. Whatever you chose was up to you. I won't judge the decision you thought was best in a horrible situation."

I swipe the tears falling down my cheeks, level my gaze with his, and swallow hard before adding, "Even if it means I terminated a pregnancy?"

"Yes. I would never expect you not to take every single precaution available." There isn't an inkling of hesitation or reluctance in his response. He's perfect in more ways than I could possibly list.

He shifts slightly without moving his arm that is supporting me and pulls out his phone. "Are you okay with inviting my family to the triple date cookout instead of dinner tonight?"

I agree with a slight nod. He put me and our relationship first. Not once has any man done that for me before.

The phone rings, and a female voice answers.

"Please tell Mom something came up and we can't make dinner tonight. We would like all of you to join us in a few weeks at my place instead."

Essie's words are too faint for me to hear.

"Yes, we're fine." There's a short pause. "I promise on old man Parker's jacket."

I frown at the reference, but he ends the call setting his phone aside. "You don't want to know?" My voice is soft and barely audible.

"Having the information will only make me want to kill him on your behalf, but if you want to share, I'll listen."

Pursing my lips, I reply, "Not more than I have."

"The only detail I need is whether this man… no… he doesn't deserve that title. Is this male in prison?"

"He is. I wasn't his only victim. Five of us testified, and he is serving a lengthy sentence."

"Good. I didn't know you then like I do now, but I'm proud of you for standing up for yourself."

"Thank you." I lean forward and press my lips to his. The same heat is present, but sharing some of my concerns makes this kiss seem freer and less inhibited. "At first, I didn't even allow Scarlett or Willa physically close to me forget a man who was basically a stranger. I had extra locks on my front door. That part was more about me regaining control. I never felt unsafe here. I haven't been with anyone since. Never considered it… until your touch made me want to succumb to bliss again."

Alden presses his lips to my forehead. Before adding space, he whispers, "I understand completely. I have only been with Asha and never wanted anyone the way I want you."

My heart pounds faster at his revelation. We feel the same about each other. As heavy as being with Alden seemed to be, the depth of our feelings added to it a bit more. On top of our revelations, we're both exhausted. It isn't until the next day we move forward physically and emotionally

CHAPTER TWENTY

ALDEN

After our discussion last night, Carly and I fell asleep in the chair. Hours later, I carried her to the bedroom and snuggled beneath her ultra-soft sheets. Craning my neck to see the clock, I note it doesn't match with the lack of sunlight streaming through her windows. It's past seven, and the room is still pitch-black. Then I recall the forecast for the day is dark and stormy. Before our discussion yesterday, that would be an apt description for my fear of speaking with Carly about sex. Now I feel lighter and prepared to move forward.

As if she is aware I'm awake and staring at her, Carly's light blue eyes meet mine. "Morning."

"Hi." I slide my hand forward, curl it around her lower back, and haul her against me.

A little squeak falls from her lips before I kiss her deeply. My palm glides over the curve of her waist and hips, searching for the hem of her dress. The heat of her skin beneath my hands is otherworldly. I push upward, drawing her dress with me. She shivers as I pull it off. Carly's breath hitches as I expose her ample breasts. I lower my head and drag my tongue along the curve of her breasts and follow a path southward.

Her hands move to lift my shirt, but I stop her by setting my hands over hers. Questions dance in her eyes.

"We need to go slow, Carly."

Her fingertips drift down my chest, leaving tingles behind, even through my shirt.

I slide one hand around her jaw and tilt her head up. I splay the other on her back. Her eyes drift closed as she wets her lips. I follow the same path before exploring the depths of her mouth. Twisting, I hover over her. I drag my tongue over her chin and down the column of her neck. Carly's chest rises and falls quicker as I move southward. Goose bumps erupt everywhere I set my lips.

When I reach the lace of her panties, I nip near her hip. Her back arches into me, and I repeat the move again but a bit harder. I trace the edge of her panties inward toward her center, and the scent of her arousal envelopes me. I hook the sides and draw the silky fabric down her legs. Skimming my fingers upward, I grip her thighs, widening them a bit. Her hands fist the sheets.

I meet her gaze. "Do you want me to stop?"

Again, she shakes her head ever so slightly.

"I need words, please."

"No." Her eyes pin on mine.

"If you change your mind, just say so."

"Alden, please." Her plea makes my chest tighten.

Drawing my finger from the bottom to the top, I spread her folds. Immediately I drag the flat of my tongue along the same course. Carly's hands thread into my hair. I lavish attention on her most intimate parts, alternating between licking, sucking, and nipping until her thighs shake and an orgasm cascades through her.

"Alden." My name falls from her lips, dripping with aching need.

The instant I spear her with my fingers and suck her clit into my mouth, she writhes against me. I slide my free hand up and remove hers from my hair, intertwining our fingers. As her release subsides, I withdraw and kiss my way upward.

She pulls her hand from mine and draws my tee over my head before resting her hands on my sides. Her breathing is slowing, but her mind is still racing. I can see her thoughts playing out on her face. She opens her eyes as her arms slide between us. Deftly, she slips her hand beneath the waistband, surrounds my shaft, and strokes me twice.

My mind, heart, and libido are racing. I'm bereft when she removes her hand from my length. The hollow feeling is short-lived. Carly pushes my shorts and boxer briefs to my feet.

I cage her beneath me and lower my lips to hers again. This kiss is deeper and measured only in passion and love. Words I'm terrified to say out loud even after sharing the only detail she didn't yet know about my sexual history. While I do, she sets kisses along my jaw and along my neck as her hand strokes my length.

"Why did you wait so long?" she whispers.

"I wasn't ready to date, let alone give myself to another woman. You?"

"No one felt right before now... before you. And now?" Carly murmurs.

"I'm ready for it to be you for the rest of my life."

"Me too."

"Any chance you have condoms?"

Her lips pull into a tight line. "No, but I have an IUD, and I haven't...."

She didn't need to share that last part. Bare our first time. I can only hope to hold out long enough.

I shifted over her. She widens her legs more to accommodate me. As I settle in, the tip of my shaft grazes her heated center. Carly's eyes snap closed, and she exhales sharply. One of her hands is at my neck while the other is over my heart. Inch by inch, I push forward slowly, watching her carefully. When I'm fully seated, I pause, and she blows out a harsh breath. The tightness of her wrapped around me is indescribable. Waiting for Carly was the right choice.

"Are you okay? Any pain?"

"Yes, but it's minimal."

I withdraw slowly and thrust back into her. This time is easier, and I can feel her inner walls spasming around me. I increase the speed of my movements and feel myself lengthen and get harder. I wasn't aware that was possible. Carly wraps her legs around me, drawing me deeper.

"Holy hell!" I'm not going to last much longer.

Her fingernails mark my back as her muscles tighten around me even more. I don't have a lot of information to go on, but her facial expression and the half-moon indentations in my skin indicate she's close too. Carly pulses around me as I explode. I struggle to find the appropriate words... that was fast, intense, and perfect.

I withdraw slowly and lower myself on top of her before turning us onto our sides. Tucking a stray hair behind her ear, I watch her replay the last minutes over in her head. Her mouth purses, then turns up into a cute smile. I drop a kiss on her forehead before curling her into my embrace.

I don't know how long we held one another, but unspoken words pass between us as if we said them aloud. I'm going to spend the rest of my life making Carly happy.

When her stomach growls, we both laugh and clean up before I prepare a late breakfast.

"Did you have plans today?" she asks over tomato and spinach omelets with bacon and toast.

"Not today. Other than work and my commissions, each moment of my time is yours."

She smiles and leans over the table for a kiss. I happily oblige. "Same for me."

After eating, we check the weather and determine a day inside is called for. I purposely ignore my messages until after our breakfast dishes are clean. My sister is still worried about us bailing on dinner last night.

Essie: Are you sure?

Me: I promise.

Essie: We will be there on Saturday.

Me: Looking forward to it.

When I realize she doesn't have ingredients for dinner, we place a delivery order.

"This is amazing. We should do this more often."

I frown. "Grocery shop?"

"Um. Yeah. Until you, I picked up my dinner and brought it home. I rarely have food in my fridge."

Inwardly, I groan. How does she look that good eating takeout all the time? "Not only can you order same day, but you can set up deliveries up to six days in advance. Speaking of which, what do we want to serve at the cookout? Do your friends have any allergies?"

Carly shakes her head. We prepare a menu, and she offers to purchase the beer and wine. "I can help cook as well, if you'll let me."

"I'm sure there will be a salad that you can handle or a no-bake dessert."

"Hardy har har." We spend the rest of the day watching action movies and laughing at the impossible stunts in between planning our cookout for next weekend.

CHAPTER TWENTY-ONE

CARLY

While I'm accustomed to the firefighter schedule, it doesn't make the fact I have to work daily any easier. Having Alden clad in only his boxer briefs in my bed as the alarm blares doesn't help either. Well, not to increase my desire to leave his sculpted chest and strong arms.

Reluctantly, I kiss him and pad to my en suite to get ready. When I leave the bathroom, Alden is no longer in my bed. He's making noise in the kitchen. An egg sandwich and a piping hot tea in a travel mug are waiting me when I join him.

"I could get used to waking up with you.'"

He hauls me against his bare chest. Flashes of yesterday ping through my mind. I knew when he kissed me, we would be fantastic together. Our first time was above average, not that I have a lot to compare it to. Either way, it can only get better, and it was....

"Maybe we can figure something out. Get going, or you'll be late. We can't have that. I'll see you later."

I rise on my toes and kiss him deeper than I should, given the time. He ushers me out my front door with my food and tea in hand. Hurrying to my car, I speed to work. I found an appointment with Willa at eleven in my inbox upon my arrival. *I wonder what that's about.* I reply "Yes" and make my way to the emergency room floor.

Since the new contract, my staff has been more pleasant and jovial not only with one another but with the patients. I hope it lasts. I greet them. Once pleasantries are out of the way, I review the charts of the remaining patients from yesterday at the nurses' station. I note a young woman with symptoms that meet a variety of diagnoses.

I seek out the staff member who took over this patient's care. "Morning, Mikel."

"Hey. How can I help you?"

"I read the data for the patient in three. Why haven't you ordered an ultrasound or CT or labs?"

He puts his hand on his hip and replies, "I followed protocol. She doesn't have any of the demarcations for appendicitis or an obstruction."

I purse my lips and calm myself. "I see the date of her last menstrual period is blank as are the questions about potential pregnancy."

Recognition of the error registers on his face. "I didn't do the intake."

"Did your review her file before speaking with her this morning?"

Mikel drops his head and mutters, "No."

Angry, I manage to say, "Follow me." I walk to the curtained area and find the young woman curled in fetal position. "Hi, Stacia. I'm Carly. I can see you're in a fair amount of pain. Could you be pregnant?"

She looks over at the man with her. "Maybe."

"Mikel, go get a new IV bag and a dose of tramadol."

I spend the next twenty minutes working with the patient. I give her pain medication, order a repeat set of labs, and schedule an ultrasound as well as complete her chart.

When I'm about to leave, she takes my hand and says, "Thank you. Neither of the guys I saw listened to me."

"You're welcome. I'll be back after you have an ultrasound and your labs are processed."

The relief on her face is palpable. I find Mikel with his head in his hands at the desk.

"Please don't fire me," he states loudly.

The last thing I want is to deplete the staff, but his failure may warrant firing or at least reprimand. I move closer to him and in a quiet voice I reply, "I can't make any promises. What were you thinking?" He opens his mouth, but I cut him off with a raised hand. "Don't answer that. I will review the case in its entirety and figure out the best course of action."

"Yes, Carly."

Angry and worried more things were missed, I finish my review of the patients from Saturday as well. Nothing of note at this point. I understand. My staff are human, but this job requires a standard of care that everyone deserves regardless of their gender or presenting symptoms.

Slightly more than an hour later, Stacia's labs show a low HCG level, which is the hormone that indicates pregnancy. The ultrasound showed an ectopic pregnancy. She's being prepped for emergency surgery. Rather than stew on the details of her case right now, including potential discipline for Mikel, I ride the elevator to Willa's office.

Unease washes over me. I have no idea what this meeting could be about. The contract has been agreed upon and my staffing levels are on point. She couldn't possibly know about Stacia. Could she?

I take a deep breath and knock on her office door.

"Come in, Carly." Her greeting doesn't sound ominous.

I step inside and latch the door behind me. "Hey, Willa. Everything okay?"

My beautiful and glowing friend frowns and tilts her head in question. "Of course. What would be… is there something you need to share?"

"Not yet. What's up?"

"Happy birthday, my friend."

"Thank you," I reply but I bristle at her words internally. I'm not a big fan of my birthday. A fact my besties are well aware of. It's the reason I didn't share with Alden yet. It isn't a big deal to me. When I was young, we didn't celebrate, so now I see it as any other day on the calendar.

Willa slides a stack of papers across her desk toward me.

"Statement of Change. These forms are executed when someone is fired or moves depart…. Really?"

Willa smiles widely. "Congrats, my sweet friend. You are now the supervising nurse of the NICU. Well, once you sign those and pick a start date. The board determined that an internal hire for that position made the most sense. I'll post your current job as soon as you sign."

A wave of happiness and accomplishment courses through me. I can't wait to share with Alden. Finally, I'll be working on my dream floor in my hometown. "Is tomorrow too soon?"

Willa laughs. "Probably. Maybe Monday?"

I take the pen she extended in my direction. Before signing, I glance at the terms. Not only is there a five percent raise but also an additional week of vacation. Nice. I input my last day as this Friday in the emergency room and hurriedly add my signature on the line.

"I'm crazy excited for you."

"Me too. How are you feeling? How many more days until the wee one joins us?"

Willa smiles. "I'm hoping in enough time for me to have him or her and attend the ball."

"Completely understand. It's a great evening out for adults only. Which sibling is lucky enough to have baby duty?"

"Ellie with supervision from Frankie if the baby is born." Frankie is one of Luca's sisters. Ellie is her stepdaughter. She's a sophomore at York High, if I recall correctly.

"Makes sense."

There's a knock on the door.

"Expecting someone?" I ask.

"Nope."

I rise from the chair and answer the door. On the other side, I find my gorgeous boyfriend with a massive bouquet of red roses.

"Hi, sweetheart," Alden greets me. He kisses me lightly and then waves to my bestie. "Willa."

"Hey, Alden," she replies.

I accept the blooms and raise them to my nose. "Thank you for the flowers. What are you doing here?"

"Someone forgot to share her birthdate with her boyfriend." His accusing gaze is pointed at me.

I draw my lips into a straight line. Truly, he's beyond words. "It isn't a day I celebrate. Never did as a child and don't now."

"Everyone deserves an exceptional meal and a cake. Plus, it's nonnegotiable for me."

"You really don't…."

He shakes his head. "I won't budge on this. I'll pick you up for dinner at 6:15. It's kind of fancy, so a sexy dress is preferable."

"Okay." There's no point in arguing with him.

Shock shows on his chiseled jaw. "Where can I find Carly Reed?"

I smile and kiss him tenderly. "I'm right here. However, I need to get moving back to my floor and start an exit memo."

"You got the job?" Alden bends at the knees, lifts me, and turns in a small circle in Willa's office.

He always hears me. It's an amazing departure from my exes.

Alden adds, "Another milestone we can celebrate tonight."

I recall we have an audience. It's my bestie but still. I whisper near the shell of his ear, "Please put me down."

He clears his throat and sets me on the floor.

"Go. I've got work to do and apparently a hot date tonight," I state.

He nods. "Bye, Willa." With a kiss to my forehead, he disappears as fast as he arrived.

I've barely recovered from the short visit when Willa's voice interrupts my glee.

"Can I say it now?"

Shaking my head, I turn to face her. "Please don't. It wasn't time before. Our window as a couple is now and for years into the future. The wait was worth it."

"I'm crazy happy for you, Car. Get moving. Love you."

A huge smile widens on my face. "Me too. Love you." I scoop up the roses and hustle to my office. I spend almost the remainder of the day drafting a memo to my staff, my incoming successor yet to be named, and reviewing Stacia's chart from beginning to end. As the clock strikes the end of the day, I'm unlocking my driver door.

I don't think Alden realizes how long it takes for a woman to get dressed for a night out, especially at a fancy restaurant. For me, forty minutes is tight. Somehow I pull off showering, drying my hair, and applying makeup with five minutes to spare before he rings my doorbell.

My mouth goes dry when I find Alden clad in a pinstripe, charcoal suit on the other side of my front door. I know my man is hot, and he looks exceptional in his dress uniform. This is an entirely different level of sexy.

"Damn, woman! Are you trying to get me to cancel our reservation?"

I frown. "No, what are you…"

He steps into the house and closes the door with his foot. "This hot-as-hell dress says otherwise."

I opted for my little black dress that has black sequin accents along the neckline. It's fitted but not tight.

His hands cup my face, and Alden kisses me deeply. Immediately, I relax in his hold, and prickles of awareness spark from my lips to my toes. We move deeper into my house. I restrain myself from pushing his jacket off his shoulders but barely.

Alden stops abruptly near the island and pulls out his phone. "Good evening, I have a reservation in twenty minutes. Is there any way I can push it until eight?"

I hear muffled words.

Then he replies, "Great. Thank you for the accommodation. We appreciate it."

"Whatever shall we do with our extra time?" My tone is intentionally sultry.

Alden looks left, then right, as if we aren't alone, and murmurs, "I'm going to make you scream."

My mouth drops open. No words can express the surprise and anticipation swirling through me. "Promise?"

"Hell yes!" Alden slips off his jacket and lays it on the chair. His lips meet mine, and I open for him. Our tongues tangle and fight for supremacy.

Alden's fingers deftly find the zipper of my dress, and he draws it down my back. Tucking his hand beneath the straps, he pushes my dress forward.

"No bra?" His question is strangled with lust and an attempt at restraint.

"No panties either," I admit while allowing the satin dress to fall to the hardwood floor.

Now it's his turn to be speechless. Alden stares unabashedly while still dressed. I see his throat move, and he swallows hard before asking, "Do you frequently skip undergarments for special events?"

I wink. "Sometimes."

With finesse and quickness, he sheds his button-down, pants, and boxer briefs. He hauls me close, trapping his impressive erection between us.

"I don't think slow is possible right now," he states.

"So don't go slow."

A torrent of heat smolders in his gaze. Alden kisses me deeply and nudges my thighs open with his leg. He plunges two fingers into me.

"You're soaked."

Breathlessly, I state, "Always, with you."

His hand moves with a frenzied pace. Jolts of naughty pleasure rumble in my abdomen. The combination of his sensual strokes and the pressure from his thumb on my swollen clit has ripples of passion radiating through me.

"Alden."

Before the waves subside, he withdraws his skilled hand and bends me over the arm of my couch. Widening my stance, he drags his hand between my legs before thrusting to the hilt. Rather than slamming into me again, he waits for me to stretch and accommodate his thick length. The tenderness is appreciated.

"Alden, I need you to…."

He pulls out and then buries himself deep inside me. One of his large hands slides around me, cupping my breasts.

The glimmer of a second orgasm forms and intensifies. Until him, I've never climaxed more than once. Most times I didn't come at all. The surging pleasure pulls me out of my thoughts. Gripping the fabric, my heart shatters into tiny pieces for this man as we fall off a cliff into joint bliss.

When the palpitations subside and our breath regulates, he withdraws and turns me in his embrace.

I meet his gaze. I expect to find regret or concern. I find neither.

"Are you okay? he asks before I can pose the same question.

"Absolutely. There are no words to describe that other than perfection. Why were you worried?"

His chocolate eyes meet mine. "Your past. I assumed…."

I shake my head. "I shared because of my choice."

He drops his forehead against mine. "Okay. Do you still want to go to dinner?" he asks while lazily dragging his fingers down my side.

"Won't you have to pay for it either way?"

He nods.

"Then we should clean up and hurry to our reservation. Where did you pick?"

"Clay Hill Farm."

I crane my neck and determine we can make it. "Let's move."

In record time, we wash up and get dressed for dinner. The ride is relatively short. The gracious staff seats us upon our arrival without an inkling that Alden spent the last hour making me scream his name. Thank goodness my neighbors are hard of hearing.

We order drinks and appetizers, including burrata and Caesar salad. The ambiance here is wonderful. It's a family-owned establishment with charm and natural elegance. Plus, the food is delicious.

We place the rest of our order after our beverages and small plates are delivered. Alden is scowling.

"What's wrong?"

"Piper just arrived."

I resist turning to locate her. "Alden."

He meets my gaze over the table as I cover his hand with mine. As I do, Piper and her date pass our table. When I realize who her date is, I'm surprised. Xander Greyson is one of the honorees for the matchmakers. We've had trouble selecting for him because he's young and has the reputation of being a playboy. From the look of him with Piper, we simply didn't select in the correct age bracket. She's at least fifteen years his senior. Nothing wrong with an age gap, but her son is not much younger than her date.

Our server refills our waters and delivers our entrées. I selected the pork tenderloin, and Alden opted for the braised short rib.

"Let's change the subject. How did you figure out today is my birthday?"

"I was looking for paper to leave you a note and found your license renewal in the kitchen drawer. It expires today."

"Eek! I'll renew it online when I get home."

"Then I texted Landry to confirm before ordering your flowers and reserving this table."

"Thank you. We didn't acknowledge this day when we were young."

His lips pull into a tight line. He disagrees wholeheartedly. "A birthday is the only moment on a calendar that belongs to one person. It begs attention. As I said before, it's nonnegotiable for me."

"I'll get used to it going forward. When is yours?"

"February 1st."

We finish our meals and order crème brûlée.

"To go, please," Alden says. From the look on our servers' face, carryout of that particular menu item isn't frequently requested.

I raise an eyebrow in question after she leaves the tableside. "Why to go?"

"I have a gift for you. It wasn't intended for your birthday, but it's finished."

When the dessert arrives, Alden hands our server his card. She returns promptly, and we leave the restaurant.

Intrigue and potential gifts float through my thoughts during the ride home, like a necklace or books or massage gift card.

Alden parks in my driveway, and we enter the house. He grabs utensils from the kitchen and a blanket off the couch.

"Where and when did you hide it?"

A devilish grin appears on his face. "While you were at work. I was fairly confident you wouldn't stumble upon it given your time constraints to get ready."

"Plus, we were otherwise occupied."

"Was that a complaint?"

I rise on my toes and press my lips to his before replying, "Hell no."

He shifts the blanket over his arm while clutching dessert and the spoons in one hand, and he takes mine in the other. "Close your eyes, beautiful."

I hesitate but comply.

Alden leads me outside to my patio. "Take a look."

No one has ever given me more than him. It isn't about the flowers and gifts. I'm here for it, but I don't need them. It's the... making sure I'm eating and demanding a celebration of me today. He's one of a kind. I'm grateful for our chance to be together all these years later. Once I gather the courage, I follow his instructions. Before me there are two Adirondack chairs with a small table between them facing toward the wooded area behind my house.

"Oh, Alden. These are fantastic! You built these for me?" I pepper him with kisses and then drag my hand along the smooth arm and take a seat.

"I did." He leans down and skims his lips across mine.

We share the crème brûlée and talk on my new patio set for longer than acceptable on a workday. Then again, I have only three more days in the emergency room. A little sleep deprivation will be fine to allow myself to enjoy my birthday for the first time ever.

CHAPTER TWENTY-TWO

ALDEN

My arms cut through the warm water as I span the length of the pool. For the first time my thoughts don't follow their usual pattern. Carly crosses my mind. The change is a prime example of my feelings for her. Feelings I should verbalize soon. Instead of attributes of my wife and daughter, I focus on my future with Carly. Being in the water is relaxing and refreshing. I haven't gotten into the water without a therapeutic goal in years… until today.

After a short swim, by my standards at least, I get ready to tackle my shift at the firehouse.

Me: Good morning, sweetheart.

Carly: Hi. Have a great day.

Me: You too.

When I arrive, the station is calm. It doesn't last long though. The tones sound just before eight.

The information pipes through the station and our radio system. "Structure fire at 123 Pine Street. Number of occupants unknown."

"Rhodes for dispatch. Show Engine 4 and Rescue 8 responding," I state over the radio.

"Roger. Station 9 en route as well," he responds.

When we arrive, flames are evident through the rear of the home with the attic engulfed.

I hop off the rig and bark out orders. "Collings and…." I hesitate for a few seconds before finishing, "… Reed, make entry. Clear the home thoroughly and expeditiously. Foster and Madden, run a line and start knocking that down from the exterior." I can't decide assignments on this job because of my feelings for Carly. I chastise myself.

"Roger, Cap," they reply and carry out my orders.

After prying the door open, they don their masks and enter through the front door. I hear them moving through the first floor.

Reed shouts, "Fire Department, call out!"

Then Collings repeats as they clear the floor.

I turn and speak with LT Borden from Rescue 8. "Please get two guys with a secondary line on the east side of the structure."

Borden nods. "Roger."

"Cap."

"Go, Reed," I answer.

He updates me on the situation inside the house, "First floor clear, advancing to second floor."

"Roger." I then speak with the firefighters at the back of the building. "Rear status."

Madden responds, "Roof line fully involved. Hose efforts leading to minimal progress."

Worry ripples through me. Being in charge means making tough decisions. It takes everything in me not to pull them out of the building immediately. I know the pain of that kind of loss. I wouldn't wish it on my worst enemy let alone Carly or my crew's family members.

"Collings, report."

"Located adult female. Exiting now."

Shouting over my shoulder, "Booker. Ransom. Victim one forthcoming." Vaughn and Auberon are also standing by with a second ambulance.

They move closer to the sidewalk with the gurney, and Booker assists Collings as he emerges from the smoke-filled property.

"My daughter. My daughter! You can't leave her!" The woman is hysterical as Booker checks her vitals.

Ransom soothes her and brings the oxygen to her face. "Breathe, ma'am. Let the firefighters do their jobs."

"Cap, still searching for the little girl," Reed states over the radio.

I drag my hand down my face. "Madden, update."

"The roof is unstable. Evacuate now." His voice echoes in my ear.

"Found her! Exiting the structure now," Reed states.

"Make it fast. The roof is unstable." Before I take my next breath, the roof collapses. Fear and the urge to hurl has me setting my hand on the engine for support.

I pull myself together a bit. "Reed! Report!" I shout, though it's unnecessary. It did make me feel a little less unhinged though.

The seconds tick by with no response. The crew beside me are stock-still as well. Nearly a minute has gone by without a peep from Landry.

"Reed, what's your status?" As I wait, I unclip the radio and rummage through the compartment for my rebreather. "Borden." Fear rushes through my veins. I can't be the reason Carly loses her brother.

"Yeah, Cap," he states as he moves closer.

"I'm going in. You're in command of the scene."

"Sir…."

I don't give him the opportunity to question my decision. I charge toward the house. "Reed! Status!" I request once more before climbing the front staircase.

"We're trapped! The roof collapse blocked our egress via the staircase. I'm clearing a path. Need evacuation assistance on the east side of the house. I can climb onto the roof of the sun porch and lower the child down."

"Roger." I request a ladder and straps to the east side of the building. Borden sends two of his crew, Rodriguez and Martins, and they set up the rescue apparatus against the lowest part of the porch. Too much time has passed, and I call out to Reed again. "Status."

I glance at my watch and wait for an answer. Nearly five minutes tick by without a response. When I reach the side porch, Landry appears with a small girl clutched against his chest and wearing his mask in the second-story window.

That explains why he didn't answer. He couldn't hear me because he removed his mask. Against protocol but…. I probably would've done the same thing in his situation. Martins straddles the peak of the roof and takes the victim from Reed. Landry swings one leg out of the window and descends the ladder. He hurries to catch up to Martins, who places the victim on the gurney with her mother. I follow closely behind.

Ransom removes Reed's mask and attempts to hand it to him. The mask falls to the concrete. My arms collapse around Landry to prevent him from hitting the ground. Foster throws Reed's arm around his shoulder, and we carry him to the ambulance.

Vaughn has an oxygen mask ready as we lift him onto the gurney.

This is my fault. I shouldn't have sent him inside.

Carly.

Protocol is for the EMTs to inform the hospital, and I'm sure they will. As Foster closes the door and knocks twice, the rig peels away.

Without thinking more, I call the ER.

"York Memorial Emergency department. How can I direct your call?"

"This is Captain Rhodes of the YFD. I need to speak with Carly Reed immediately." I hope to convey urgency but not fear.

"One moment please."

I listen to the hold music and attempt to figure out what I'm going to say. "A roof collapsed on your brother, and he isn't breathing well" is not the best choice.

"Good morning, Carly speaking."

I clear my throat. "Landry was injured on our call. He's on his way to you. He gave his mask to the tiny victim. I'm so sorry."

Her response is eerily calm, unmistakably flat and emotionless. "Not your fault. We'll be ready." The line goes silent.

My chest tightens, and I can't breathe myself for a moment. It is a most inopportune time for me to realize... I love her. I broke our firmly established protocol by handing command over to Borden. I'm not managing the scene appropriately. I'm also considering ways to hand it off to get to her. I will do anything for her, even shirk my responsibilities to my crew, which doesn't include me charging into a structure anymore. I'm head over heels in love with Carly Reed. A deeper renewed interest in the future has me hiding a smile.

"Cap." One of my crew pulls me out of the thoughts.

I exhale and answer, "Go for Rhodes."

"The flames have been drowned," Madden informs me.

"Roger. Verify for hot spots then secure the area." He means the crew surrounded the flames and put them out.

"Will do."

I survey the scene and confirm that YPD has cordoned off the street. They will only allow access for locals until the structure is released by the investigation unit.

Nearly an hour after the ambulances left the scene, I climb into the truck and return to the firehouse. Cleaning up is the last thing on my mind. Once the truck is parked, I give orders to the crew and make my way to York Memorial to check on Reed.

I hustle inside, despite knowing it's unnecessary. Landry is clearly already being seen given the time that passed. At reception, I greet Millie.

"Captain Rhodes. Bay three," she states, then buzzes me in. First responders aren't left in the waiting room.

When I arrive, Carly is standing at the edge of the room. I was unable to remove myself as far as monitoring Landry. It appears Mikel and Janie removed Carly.

My stunning and patient woman turns as I approach. I stop beside her and look in on Reed.

"Carly, I'm—"

She shakes her head. As if magnets are sewn into our palms, Carly threads her fingers with mine. "Not now. Not here. Landry is going to be fine." Her gaze shifts from her brother up to me.

I expect ire, frustration, and fear in her eyes. I don't find any of those emotions. A sliver of concern is evident perhaps. I'm hoping her taking my hand is a good sign that she isn't harboring any anger toward me.

Janie finishes making notes in Reed's chart and walks toward the exit. "He has moderate smoke inhalation. We gave him oxygen through the cannula and Albuterol to relax his airways. He should be good to go home at the end of the day with supervision from you for the next two days. You can go in as his sister only."

"Thanks, Janie. I'll keep my hands off his chart and meds."

"Much appreciated." The petite woman smiles and walks toward the nurses' station.

Mikel leaves with a nod, and we enter the room. Carly stares at her brother as if he intends to bull-rush her and leave the hospital.

"I'm fine, Car. Just a little too much smoke in my lungs. Cap."

I nod. "Up to telling me what happened?"

"Foster located the mom and egressed. I continued my search. Mariella was under the bed in the guest bedroom. When I heard the cracking sounds of the roof, I forcibly dragged her from under the bed and rushed into the hallway." Landry coughs a few times.

Carly squeezes my hand. I'm not sure if it means "this is your fault" or "I need comfort." I'm desperate for it to be the latter, but the former is more likely.

He continues, "As I closed the door behind us, the roof collapsed. I shielded her against the wall. When I could assess, I determined the stairs were no longer an option." Landry clears his throat and takes a sip of water. "I answered your status call. Removed my mask and put it on Mariella. Don't yell. She's so tiny. I broke the rules. I know. Then I cleared a narrow path to the bathroom at the end of the hall for egress. You know the rest."

Carly looks up at me in interest.

Reed asks, "What were you doing on the east side of the property prepared to make entry?"

I shake my head. I refuse to divulge my reasons before I share my feelings with Carly.

Landry drinks more water after coughing again.

"Why don't you get some rest?" Carly suggests. "I'll be back in a little bit."

"Go easy on him, sis." Reed chuckles and then catches his breath.

"Alden, follow me," Carly demands.

I have no chance or inkling to ignore her.

Without missing a beat, she leads me directly to the elevator. In silence, we ride upstairs, and my apparently upset girlfriend leads me down the carpeted hall to her office. Her footfalls give her emotions away… or at least I think so.

She swipes her badge and enters her office. The door snicks closed. "Why?"

"Why what?"

"You broke protocol," she states with her hand on her hip like when we first met. The stance was hotter when the fiery words weren't aimed at me.

"I did." I take a step closer to her. Using my finger under her chin, I lift her head.

"Because?" The word is soft and laced with worry.

I swallow hard. I only shared this sentiment with one other woman in my entire life. Losing a second chance at happiness would destroy me. "I love you. I needed to tell you myself that Landry was injured on my watch."

She stares at me wordlessly for nearly a minute. "Promise me you will never put me above your duty again."

"I can't do that. When I love, I do it hard, deep, and above everything else, including myself and my guys. Is that wrong? Perhaps. In a perfect world, I'll never have to make this decision again. Once is enough."

Her lips are in a tight line, and I'm afraid she won't reciprocate my feelings. "I love you, Alden."

Despite being sweaty, dirty, and covered in grime from the scene, I surround her in my arms and seal our admission with a toe-curling, knee-buckling kiss for the ages. I loved Asha, but it was different than how I love Carly. My first love was sweet and tender. My forever love is all encompassing and spectacular.

"What happens now?"

"We make plans for our future together."

She wrinkles her button-nose. "What kind? How far are we talking?"

"For starters, I would like to wake up with you when I'm not working. We can look for somewhere to live together."

"Are you up for sharing your home with me? I have conditions."

Will it bother me to share the space I bought for Asha with Carly? To allow Carly to use the closet I built for my wife? I'm surprisingly not freaking out. That fact is comforting. To me it means I'm in control of my feelings and ready to move forward with my life. "What kind of conditions?"

"More color, pillows and blankets… everywhere."

I shake my head. "What else? I know there's more."

"Can we find a spot for my birthday gift?"

"Of course. When I'm off shift, I'll show you the perfect location to read and watch sunrise and sunset."

"Then I'm in," she replies.

I lift her again and turn in a small circle. The space in her office isn't large. After a kiss that is close to inappropriate, I press my lips to her forehead. I don't miss the sigh it causes.

"I have to go. We can coordinate in a few days. Maybe this weekend before the barbecue?"

She smiles and replies, "Okay. Call me later. Love you. Be safe."

I step toward the door. "I will. I love you." I exit before I don't return to the station and even more questions are asked. I don't make a habit of checking on the victims of a call anymore. Earlier in my career, I did, but it was never for them. It was always for me. On my way out, I look in on Landry again.

"All good with Carly?" he asks.

I can feel my face heating up. Thankfully, Landry is none the wiser. "Yeah, we're good. Listen to your doctors."

"You got it, Cap."

Hurrying back to the house, I shower and then write up the report for the call. As much as I would like to protect myself, I set forth the truth as well as recommend Landry for a commendation. He made smart, quick decisions. While he didn't follow procedure to the letter, he probably helped Mariella to his own detriment by giving up his mask.

Hours later as the day winds down, I text Carly.

Me: Have an update for me?

Carly: I'll take Landry to my place for a few days to keep an eye on him.

Me: I bet your brother will love that.

Carly: Not at all.

Me: Call me when you can. Love you.

Carly: I will. Love you.

I stare at our exchange. The words aren't hollow. I love Carly. My feelings are deeper and more intense than with Asha. I'm not disconcerted or worried. Progress is noted toward my goals. Once she's moved in, we can plan the rest of our lives together, which hopefully means starting a family sooner rather than later.

CHAPTER TWENTY-THREE

CARLY

I close the door to my guest room quietly behind me. Landry is sound asleep. I'll check on him later. He'll be fine in a few days and back to work. Blaming Alden will do me no good. My brother took a calculated risk. Aside from his break in protocol by calling me and leaving his post to rescue my brother, he didn't do anything crazy. Hopefully the brass will see that as well.

With a cup of tea, I grab a blanket to keep the bugs away and sit in my chair outside. At first, I was angry Alden called. Pondering the move while my team was caring for Landry, my ire increased. Knowing the true reason for breaking the rules, I can understand his feelings. As he said, we won't have to revisit a call like that again.

I'm a few days from starting my dream job, my boyfriend loves me, and we're moving in together. On the outside it seems fast, but I've known Alden my entire life. The timing wasn't right until now, and waiting some arbitrary, societally acceptable timeframe to share living space seems silly to me.

A few hours later, my doorbell chimes. I rise from the chair and answer the door.

"Mia." Where was she today? "Please come in. Did Landry call you?"

"Yes. I was at my grandmother's funeral. He was covering my shift, and he got hurt. I rushed back as fast as I could." She's visibly shaken by Landry's injury.

"Please don't blame yourself. I can't have both of our better halves shouldering guilt from today. Landry was doing his job. He saved a little girl. Speaking as a nurse who happens to be his sister, he will be fine."

"Thank you. Can I see him?"

"Of course. Down the hall, second room on the left." The instant she has the door open enough to see Landry, her shoulders drop in relief. Rather than check his vitals now, I prepare my lunch for tomorrow and finish a load of laundry that has been sitting in the dryer for at least three days. Good thing I have two weeks' worth of scrubs and panties.

Nearly an hour later and Mia hasn't returned. I peek in on them. Landry raises his hand to his lips to shush me. Mia fell sound asleep against him. Using hand signals, I ask how he's feeling. He answers by rotating his hand. To me, that means he's "meh." Better than "blah" like he was before. I tell him Mia can stay and I'm turning in for the night. Our childhood made-up sign language still works.

I check my messages again and find one from Alden.

Alden M. Rhodes: Going on a call. Goodnight, sweetheart. I love you.

Me: Be safe. I love you.

I don't expect a reply and snuggle beneath my sheets for the night.

Thankfully, my last day on the emergency room floor is peaceful, and my staff opts for a small farewell since I'm only moving upstairs, not to a distant land. I'm grateful. I don't relish being the center of attention, at least not professionally. Alden's undivided attention is welcome and will be cherished as long as he'll have me. We are moving most of my things into his house this weekend.

Landry has been cleared to return to work for his next shift. His lungs have healed nicely, and he has no residual issues at this point. He's considering moving into my place for a rent comparable to what he's paying now with Madden. For the last time as the head nurse of the emergency department, I exit York Memorial. Excitement bubbles in my belly for a new challenge next week. As I drive home, I mentally figure out what I can bring with me tonight. Considering I haven't packed anything, and I need to meet Alden for party preparation in an hour, not much.

As quickly as possible, I throw clothes and overnight items into my tote. Alden waits for me patiently on his front porch when, despite my hustle, I'm a few minutes late. He stows my bag in the house, kisses me deeply, and we're off to pick up groceries.

This is the first time I've witnessed Alden shopping. He's methodical as he walks through the store. There isn't a list in his hands, but he seems to have one in his head. Aisle by aisle, he selects the items without missing one or backtracking. He also hasn't balked at my additions to the cart, including Twizzlers and mint chocolate chip ice cream. He's a keeper. Once the list only he can read is complete, we check out and go to his place. Soon after we arrive, the doorbell rings.

"Expecting someone?" I ask.

"Pizza," he answers with a wink.

"When did you order?"

"On my phone while you were picking your disgusting ice cream."

"I see. No problem. More for me." I happily accept the food and thank him for taking care of dinner, otherwise we would have cereal.

"Inside or outside?"

He smiles. No doubt he is recalling that I prefer to be outside, which matches his preference.

"Outside." We enjoy our dinner under the waning sunshine and the appearance of a blanket of stars. When the bugs and the chill in the air become too much, we turn in for the night.

While this evening isn't the first time I've slept over, it is the first one on purpose. I opt for the side of the bed farther from the door. Alden pauses when he returns from the en suite.

"Do you want me to switch sides?" I can't imagine this is easy for him. While it would be an assumption, the furniture looks masculine and likely not the set Asha selected.

"No. You should be away from the door."

"You're a starfish, huh?"

He grins widely. "Maybe. I'm willing to share my space with you."

"Good. Let's get some rest. We have a lot of work to do in the morning to pull off an awesome afternoon barbecue."

Alden laughs heartily. "You're only handling plating prepared foods. I can't have you making our guests sick."

"Ha ha ha. I'm not that bad."

Alden shrugs and slides beneath the sheets. I meet him in the middle and kiss him goodnight before turning and nestling against him like a small spoon. Being cocooned in his embrace is exactly where I belong.

Sunlight warms my face, but I'm cold and so are the sheets beside me. I glance at the bedside clock and notice it's nearly eight in the morning. I throw on his YFD zip-up hoodie and pad to the kitchen. Without another thought, I open the French doors and take a seat by the pool.

When Alden reaches the shallow end, he says, "Morning, sweetheart," mid-stroke and continues to the far side of the pool.

"Hi. How long have you been out here?"

"Not sure. Three more laps and I'll hit two miles."

I wrinkle my nose and do the math. "You already did over one hundred laps?"

He laughs without stopping. "That's a warm-up."

Rather than disturb him more, I watch him closely. The line of his arm cutting through the water is purposeful and strong. His legs tighten as he explodes off the wall at the turn. Who knew swimming was so hot! My ogling time doesn't last long. Alden climbs the steps. My man is sexy from behind as well. I narrowly resist the urge to fan myself.

Despite having put in a full workout, in my opinion, he prepares omelets and turkey bacon, which isn't as bad as it sounds. While we eat, he shares the schedule.

"After we arrange the tables outside, you're on décor and place settings."

I roll my eyes at him. "You were serious about keeping me away from food preparation."

"Yes. I love you, but we should work in our comfort zones. Cooking excellent food is one of mine."

I wink at him. "Fine." We finish our breakfast and arrange the tables. Alden absconds to the kitchen, and I fuss outside on the patio. When I come back into the house, it smells wonderful, and the island is covered with bowls and platters.

"Wow! That looks amazing!" I state and reach out to steal a celery stick.

Unceremoniously, he slaps my hand. "Not yet!" Then Alden gifts me his signature dimpled smile that warms me from the inside out.

"I'm going to get ready. Our guests should be here in less than an hour."

"I'll be right there."

"Who said I plan on sharing your massive shower?"

"I think it's ours now." He grins at me and finishes his task.

With that reminder I hustle to the master en suite to use the hottest water for myself. To be fair, he... we have a tankless hot water heater, so in essence he'll have hotter water. Alden steps into the glass enclosure when I'm finished washing my hair.

"Do you think joining me is a good idea?" I ask.

"Always. It's too bad I don't have enough time to ravish you properly."

Heat zips along my spine. "Promise?"

"Hell yes! I can't get enough of you, and now you will be here every morning." Alden kisses me deeply to the point of breathlessness before showering quickly.

I'm not surprised when our first guests arrive early. He hurries to answer while tugging his shirt down. With a spritz of perfume, I follow the noise. If I had to guess, Essie and her family are here.

Halston greets me first. "Hi, Miss Carly." He rushes over and hugs me.

"What's up?"

He loops his arm through mine and turns toward the patio. "We should swim like right now."

We stop before exiting the house.

"That is up to your mom, and I need to greet our other guests before I jump in."

He ponders my response and replies, "Fair. It's a date for later."

Essie meets us near the door and hugs me. "Sorry about him. You're a puzzle. He hasn't ever seen his uncle dating. He also may have a huge crush on you."

"No worries. It's sweet. I'll be out in a little while," I state, noting Alden calling me over to meet our guests.

Alden slides his arm around my waist when I'm beside him. "Carly, please meet Rafael and his husband, Mauro."

Rafael is tall and lean. His polo is a shade of teal to match his plaid golf shorts. Mauro appears more relaxed in a Nirvana tee shirt and bathing suit.

"Pleasure to meet you both."

"You left out she's beautiful, Alden."

My boyfriend kisses my temple. "Did I? Please join our other guests outside. We'll be there soon."

Mauro whispers loudly. "When do we get to grill her?"

I lean forward and reply, "Ask whatever you want."

He smiles, and they join Essie in the backyard.

The doorbell chimes once again. When we answer, I find my besties and their spouses on the other side. We greet each other, and the guys bro hug.

"Your home is lovely, Rhodes," Willa states as she sets down a chocolate confection of some kind on the island.

"Thanks. Carly put the drinks and snacks up near the pool."

"Only Gladys and Harvey left, right?" I ask.

Alden frowns. "Landry and Mia, right?"

"Yes."

He hauls me into his arms and kisses me. "Go. I'll be out soon." Once he releases me, I find we had an audience of one... Essie. Our lip-lock wasn't over-the-top but probably wouldn't have been as long or deep if we knew we weren't alone.

When I pass through the French doors, I survey the backyard. Halston and Henry are playing catch in the shallow end of the pool under the watchful eye of their father. Interestingly, Willa and Scarlett are chatting it up with Rafael.

I approach to the sounds of laughter. "How do you know each other?"

Willa smiles. "Mauro works at York Elementary as a guidance counselor. He worked with Luca and then Tino for the school resource officer program." Her husband, Luca, is with the state police now and Tino, her brother-in-law, is the officer at York High. Occasionally, they rotate through the middle and primary schools as well.

"Nice. What about you?" My question is directed at Rafael.

He smiles. "I own and operate an IT company."

Mauro raises an eyebrow. "Babe, don't be modest." He sets his hand on my forearm and adds, "My husband runs the second largest privately owned company on the East Coast."

"Next time the computers go wonky at work, I know who to call," Willa jokes.

The group laughs and continues chatting.

"Tell us a bit more about you, Carly." Rafael asks. "Alden was light on the details."

"If you weren't married, you might take a second look. I would've left out she's stunning as well," Mauro shares.

"Thank you. Until yesterday, I was the supervising nurse in the emergency department at York Memorial. Next week, I'm shifting to the same position for the NICU."

"Congrats!" Rafael offers.

I smile, and we chat more about the fact I'm a local like Alden and we've known each other since we were about six years old. A little while later, Gladys and Landry enter the house, whispering like teenage girls. I wonder what that's about. That is the second... no, third time I've seen them overly chummy. Rather than wonder, I excuse myself and greet them both.

I hug Gladys and offer a hello to my brother and Mia. "Thank you for coming. You two are all smiles. What's going on?"

Landry pauses a bit too long in my mind. He's hiding something. "We were talking about Mariella, my injury, and the award."

"What award?" I ask. I'm aware of Alden's presence before he slides his hand around me. Joy warms me from head to toe that we're finally building a life together.

"Want to share, Cap?" Landry looks up at his boss and my boyfriend.

Alden shakes his head. "You should."

"Chief Bertoni called me earlier today. It's why we were late. I'm receiving the Donovan Brown award for bravery in the line of duty."

I throw my arms around Landry. "This is exciting. When?"

"At the First In, Last Out ball."

Mia leans in and murmurs, "I guess we have to go now, huh?"

The group laughs. Although I don't blame her. While I love the idea of dressing up, networking and schmoozing isn't my idea of fun in high heels.

Landry shrugs and inwardly, I sigh. He must accept the award in person. I make a mental note to follow up with him in plenty of time. I notice Gladys looks relieved. Now I'm confident something is going on. What, I'm not sure.

We continue chatting about Landry and his award. Near the shell of my ear, Alden asks, "All good here?"

I turn my head to meet his gaze. "Yeah. Your friends are great."

"They are. Also, I may have some evidence that we were set up by your group."

My eyes widen, and I mouth, "No way."

He draws his lips into a tight line and nods.

"By who?"

Alden kisses my cheek and replies, "I'll share later. I put all the pieces together, and it makes sense, maybe."

My mind starts to spin with possibilities when I should be focused on our guests. I'm confident Willa and Scarlett wouldn't be able to maintain secrecy. Although their advice was on point but not pushy. If they were facilitating, they would've been more active in fostering our coupling. Both of them were supportive but not over-the-top. If it is them, I didn't see it coming. Mentally, I continue through the members of the group. Aside from the meetings, I don't socialize with the other members. Tatum and Zara were at the softball game, but we only spoke about the photos. Plus, the members agreed to hold off on matching me until we reopened the list. I turn slightly and stare unabashedly at my man. He's at the grill with tongs in his hand, rotating the corn spears.

"Carly." Someone snickers beside me. "Earth to Carly."

"Hmm. Sorry, what?"

"Ogling isn't polite," Scarlett scolds me in good fun.

"Says who?" *Mine.*

"Can you direct me to the bathroom?"

I grin at her. "I'll walk with you." We loop our arms together. Once we're out of earshot, I ask, "Have some news to share?"

My gorgeous, curvy bestie feigns ignorance. "Me? News?"

A look of annoyance flickers on my face.

"Auntie Carly duties are not yet required."

Sadness washes over me for my bestie. "Sorry, sweets."

"It hasn't been that long. I'm not worried yet." She slips into the bathroom. I grab a thin hoodie from our bedroom. Then I wait at the end of the hall for my friend who emerges shortly after I lean against the wall,

"What was on your mind back there?"

"Alden mentioned he thinks someone set us up. Care to fess up?"

She instantly shakes her head. "Not me. Although, if you were paired, it was seamless with perfect timing and execution."

"Right?"

"Are we trying to ferret out the culprit?"

I laugh heartily. "Not now, not tonight. Eventually, we'll figure out who pulled off the best match in book club history."

"Speak for yourself!"

"I mean the secrecy part only. Each book club couple is successful in their own way."

"Fair. Are you as happy and settled as you look?"

More so. "I am. I may have had an inkling of us long ago, but it wasn't time yet."

"I'm overjoyed for you. Love you, Car."

"Love you, Scar."

We return to the party and spend the rest of the evening talking, eating delicious food, and having a great time. Slowly, the crowd begins to dissipate around seven. Essie and her family as well as Gladys and Harvey leave in the first wave. Aside from a brief hello, I wasn't able to talk to them long. Halston and Henry were adamant about my presence in the pool. Like before, tank top included despite Alden's support otherwise.

Willa and Scarlett assist with clearing the dishes before they exit.

"Thank you for coming," I offer between hugging them both.

Willa checks left and right before saying, "I'm so excited for you and Alden. You have never been this happy. I assume it's because of him."

The fact my friends can see the pronounced effect Alden has on me is heartwarming. "It is. We have been honest, brutally so, and our goals are compatible."

"How long until we hear wedding bells for you?"

I glance over her shoulder at Alden in the kitchen adding to the pile of dishes. "Someday. Maybe. See you soon. Love you both." I wave to Luca and Zack as they escort their wives out the front door. As fast as this feels, if he asked tomorrow I would say yes. We've talked through some hard things and if we resolve to keep that going, we'll be fine. It doesn't hurt that he's a magician in the kitchen and a sorcerer in the bedroom.

Mauro has joined Alden, and they're loading the dishes and drying the large bowls and platters. Laughter surrounds them.

Rafael passes me and steps outside again. Turning back, he asks, "Can we do anything else? Moving the tables, perhaps?"

"You've done enough. We'll take care of those tomorrow." While Alden met Rafael under terrible circumstances, he's the best kind of friend— the one who stays until the cleanup is done.

Alden and Mauro finish the dishes, and we walk him and his partner to the door.

"It was a pleasure meeting you both," I share.

"You as well. Don't be strangers. We should set a dinner again soon. We'll host."

Alden threads his fingers with mine. "Deal." Our guests leave, and Alden scoops me into his arms.

I laugh heartily. "Was I too far away?"

"All day."

"Awww. I love you too. We made it through our first party."

"We did. I'm looking forward to many more."

I kiss him lightly. "Me too. Care to share your evidence that we were set up? Better yet, who do you think it was? I asked Scarlett outright, and she denied it. Plus, I would know if they were acting suspicious."

Alden laughs. "I think it was my mother."

"In Scarlett's words, the setup was seamless with perfect timing and execution. Gladys was a little too buddy-buddy with Landry on more than one occasion, including your ceremony and today. My brother begging off softball game planning did force us together. But how?"

"Perhaps Mom asked him to quit and request I replace him. You are the lead matchmaker. Your besties didn't do it, and we haven't talked to or socialized with anyone until today."

"Do we care? Do we plan on doing anything about it?"

Alden bestows a dimpled grin on me. No matter when or why, his smile gets me every single time. "Whether by design or sheer luck, the matchmakers never tried to pair me up before, at least not as far as I'm aware. I'm sure my mom had something to do with it when she was in charge."

I shake my head. "Not while I was fostering the group either. We never felt confident any of the new residents would be a good fit."

"I was determined to find someone who didn't know about my wife and daughter. Turns out, the opposite was true. I needed you… an OG local and friend from elementary school."

"It's our time now."

"Yes, it is." He leads me to the bedroom. With painstaking precision, we strip out of our clothes and snuggle in our bed. Until the wee hours of the morning, we explore and taste each other. Agreeing to a date with Alden was one of the more difficult decisions I've ever made.

Now, we're planning a life together, starting with officially moving in tomorrow.

CHAPTER TWENTY-FOUR

ALDEN

"Sweetheart, are you ready yet?" I call from the bedroom door. Carly has been in the master closet/dressing room for over an hour. Not only that, but she has also kept her gown a secret.

A snicker reverberates toward me. "Yes, but…."

I advance toward the closet. At first, I thought it would bother me having Carly use the space I built for Asha. Part of me healing is knowing my girlfriend accepts my past, and that makes me a better man. "But what?" I ask as I near the entry.

"If I leave this space too soon, we will be late for the ball."

My jaw hits the floor when I step into the master closet. Carly is a goddess in an emerald dress. The V-neck dress is beaded between her breasts and has a slit high on her thigh. Her hair falls around her face in perfect ringlets. I swallow hard and adjust myself. "You're stunning."

She meets my gaze in the reflection of the full-length mirror. "Thank you. You're sexy yourself."

I stop behind her and draw my fingertips down the elegant curve of her neck to her hand. "You're absolutely correct about leaving this dressing room too early."

Goose bumps rise on her skin. Mentally, I calculate how much time we have as I place a line of kisses across her back.

"Alden." My name sounds like a prayer falling from her lips. I could hear her voice daily for the rest of my life and be blissfully happy. As much as I would like to say I have enough restraint to walk away, I don't. I also knew it before I joined her in here. I grip the zipper on the middle of her back and lower her dress to the floor.

As if the dress itself wasn't enough, Carly is wearing matching lace lingerie. "You could've warned me." I learn something new about her each day. This image will keep me perpetually ready as long as I live.

"Where's the fun in that? I would've missed that hot-as-hell dumbstruck look on your face. We are going to have to be fast and dirty to be on time."

"Yes, ma'am."

She turns before me and drops my pants and boxer briefs to the floor before wiggling out of her thong. I take a seat on the tufted bench, and Carly straddles my thighs. Without finesse, I push inside her until I'm fully seated. She sets her hands on my shoulders, lifts off me, and plunges back down. We find our rhythm, and coils of pleasure gather at the base of my spine. Being with Carly has never been boring or the same. I lower my hand between us and tease her clit. Her inner walls pulse around me, and her body shakes as we free-fall into heaven at once.

Carly rests her forehead against mine, and we catch our breath. "If we hurry, we won't be late."

"Even if we are, it was worth every second." I kiss the tip of her nose and add space between us. "Besides, we're only going to miss the blue carpet, not the ceremony or dancing."

"True." She stands and pads to the bathroom. After cleaning up, she checks her makeup, and I zip her dress. We arrive at the venue fashionably late. By that I mean, we are the second-to-last couple to enter the event. *Worth it.*

While I love being Captain, I loathe the networking and brownnosing that comes with the title. Having Carly beside me makes the time fly by quicker. Plus, the higher-ups of the YFD aren't rude and keep the minute details to themselves. I appreciate the accommodation immensely.

When we arrive, we greet Chief Bertoni and his wife, Anna.

"The early feedback from your promotion is excellent, especially after the collapse on Pine. I was concerned when Borden's report set forth your intention to make entry," my boss states.

"I did. I'm down a crew member. I would've entered the structure if Reed didn't exit with the young girl in a few minutes." My explanation is only slightly in a gray area. I fully intended to burst into the building. Carly was the reason, not my lack of manpower. The chief doesn't need to know that tidbit though. It isn't a lie but it wasn't my main reason for considering charging into a burning building. I would make the same choice over and over. Bertoni likely isn't aware that I broke the protocol and called Carly directly after Landry's injury. I would do it again in a heartbeat. Consequences be damned.

"I'd forgotten that detail. I'll make sure Susan pushes the transfer request for Lt Bryce through first thing next week."

"Much appreciated."

The music shifts, and the lights flicker, indicating we should sit.

"It was a pleasure seeing you again, Chief."

He acknowledges Carly's statement.

She says, "Lovely to meet you as well, Mrs. Bertoni."

Anna is a heavyset woman and quite short. She turns her attention to me. "I believe you may have picked the perfect partner as you rise in the YFD ranks."

I squeeze Carly's hand. "Without a doubt. Have a wonderful evening."

The chief and his wife leave. I lean down and whisper, "Ready to take our seats?"

A shiver races down Carly's spine. "You know what that move does to me. I would rather find an empty conference room or office."

I feign shock, kiss her to the brink of impoliteness, and escort her to our table.

"'Bout time," Landry greets Carly. "You look nice though."

She looks better than nice, but he's her brother, not a man who wants to peel the dress from her body—again. My plan for as soon as we leave here.

Mia, who is seated beside him, shoots him the side-eye and says, "Lan, your sister is being an excellent girlfriend. Leave her alone."

Carly drops her head and replies, "Appreciate your support, Mia."

The staff brings out the salad course. We talk through the meal. Only when the Chief takes the podium does it become apparent that Landry is terrified.

His face is beet red, and he's tugging on his collar. "I can't do this." Landry pushes his chair back.

As he does, Mia sets her hand on his arm. "Breathe."

Carly shifts in her chair. Without question, she's monitoring his pulse and respiration from a few seats over. Her attention to people in distress is sexy as hell. Now her focus is the most vulnerable babies of our fair town. She's crushing her new job and loves it. The full circle moment isn't lost on me. Carly wanted to save Alicia. Now she has a chance to advocate for another tiny baby.

Mia continues, "You deserve recognition for saving Mariella. It wasn't a simple rescue. Easy would've been following Foster out down the stairs. You did so much more than that." She's correct. Rerouting after their original egress was blocked was quick thinking under pressure. The entire time he kept Mariella safe and calm.

Landry stares at her and blinks. He inhales deeply.

While we settle Landry, three awards have been presented. It means time is short for him to pull himself together.

A sweet voice echoes in the reception hall. "Thank you, Firefighter Reed."

Landry's gaze quickly pivots to the stage. Mariella and her parents are standing beside Bertoni.

Chief Bertoni speaks next. "For exemplary bravery and heroism under extreme circumstances, the York Fire Department presents the Donovan Brown award to Firefighter Landry Reed."

Landry scrubs his hand down his face, rises, and buttons his jacket. Mariella descends the small staircase to the stage and runs across the parquet dance floor to Reed.

"Are you nervous too?" she asks Landry, who crouches beside her.

He nods.

"I was scared in my house, and you helped me. I'll help you tonight." Mariella, clad in a blue satin dress, extends her small hand to Landry.

Reed is one of my best firefighters. He smiles and allows the sweet girl to lead him to accept his award. Bertoni presents the award, and Landry reads a short and simple self-deprecating speech about doing his job and nothing more. He's wrong there. He broke the rules by giving Mariella his mask. True, you see it frequently on television. That principle is the same as on an airplane, where adults are instructed to don their oxygen masks first.

Landry returns to the table, and we congratulate him. I'm not listening to the ceremony at all.

"… if Captain Alden Rhodes would join me up here."

I frown and look at Carly. She shakes her head, indicating she has no idea what is happening. Despite my reluctance, I heed his request.

Bertoni shakes my hand when I join him onstage. "I've had the pleasure of working with a member of your family for the entirety of my career. The same holds true for my father before me." He raises his hand, "My apologies, I skipped a step. Please welcome the Rhodes family to the stage."

I turn to my left and find my uncle, mother, sister, brother-in-law, and nephews preparing to join me onstage. Unfortunately, there are only six remaining members of the Rhodes family. Halfway up the stairs, Gladys Rhodes notices that Carly is not with me. Instead of following instructions, she crosses the dance floor and takes Carly's hand.

A few words are exchanged, but I can't hear them this far away. Regardless of the stability of our newish relationship, I would bet Carly was attempting to stay at the table. I don't take it as a bad thing. Like me, she isn't a fan of these types of events or being the center of attention. My mother wouldn't accept no as an answer.

The guests wait for the Rhodes women to take their places on stage. Marrying Carly is the next step for me. I realize the pace is alarmingly fast. However, I spent too much time as a recluse and hiding from my fears and grief. She makes me happy, and I want to build a life with her.

"Hi, gorgeous," I whisper. I kiss her cheek, and thread my fingers through hers.

She smiles and focuses her attention on Bertoni.

"As I was saying, for three-quarters of a century, a Rhodes man has been a member in this department. Recently, Alden Rhodes was promoted to Captain of Station Twenty-five. I learned that the day he was sworn in was the seventy-fifth anniversary of his great-grandfather Perry's first day on the job. To commemorate the selfless service of the Rhodes family, I present to Captain Alden Rhodes the first ever Legacy Award."

My chest tightens as he speaks. I didn't realize the date was significant. I'm glad it worked out that way.

"Congratulations, Alden," Carly says and kisses me lightly.

Then I hug my family members before accepting the plaque. The chief ushers me before the microphone. "I'm speechless. Literally, as in I did not prepare any words of thanks, as I'm shocked by this presentation. That said, I'm honored to accept this on behalf of my family but feel it was unnecessary. We are drawn to the first responder ranks and found our calling in firefighting. Thank you."

The crowd claps and rises to their feet. As a group, we leave the stage and are ushered into a small anteroom for photos. Tatum and her sister Zara are setting up a family portrait. We take one with me, my mother, and my uncle only. It makes sense. The three of us are the direct line of Rhodes fire department succession if you will. Then we take a huge photo with everyone.

We retake our seats and enjoy a chocolate truffle mousse. The DJ turns up the music, and the younger set of guests start dancing the night away.

Carly and I are the only people sitting at the table. She sets her head on my shoulder. "Did you know about the plaque?"

I shake my head. "Not at all. Uncle Stephon and my mother kept it a secret as well."

"They knew you would object," Carly astutely points out.

"True. I appreciate you joining us on stage. What did my mother say to you?"

Carly lifts her head and meets my gaze. "She said the entire family needed to be beside you."

"She was right. You are my person, and I want you with me through the good times and bad. You in?"

She leans forward and kisses me. After pulling back, Carly replies, "Yes. I'm in. I love you."

"I love you. Up for dancing, or do you want to go home?"

"One slow dance and then we leave."

I grin at her. "Deal." As luck would have it, the music tempo decreases. I wrap my arms around Carly near the edge of the dance floor. For the next three minutes, we exist alone in this room full of our friends and coworkers. I'm holding the love of my life, and I refuse to let her go.

CHAPTER TWENTY-FIVE

ALDEN

Since the ball, Carly and I have settled into living together and making our crazy schedule work for us. When I'm off from the station, we have lunch in her office at least two of the days. I've learned her favorite sandwich from Vocaturra's as well as her perfect Thai order from the village spot. The other days I've been in my workshop, building an intricate puzzle box. Yesterday, I finally finished. I have one more huge step before I propose to Carly: ask Landry for permission.

We just returned after a motor vehicle accident call near Long Sands Beach. Our presence was a precaution. When Reed exits the engine, I speak with him. "Reed, please stop by my office after you clean up and stow your gear."

"Sure, Cap."

I hang my turnout suit and grab a water from the kitchen. As soon as I wake my computer, Landry appears in my doorway.

"Come in. Please close the door."

He immediately frowns.

"You aren't in trouble."

Reed laughs. "You had me worried there for a second. I would ask about Carly, but I texted her before the call. What's up?"

Since I started dating Carly, divulging my feelings has been improving. My heart is pounding as I try to come up with the right words. "I realize your sister is an adult. She may think this practice is archaic, but I'm a traditional guy. Given what Carly shared about your family—"

"So you want to marry my sister?" he asks pointedly.

My failure to speak well didn't hamper this conversation. I'm grateful. "Yes."

"Are you sure?" His tone leads me to believe his question is sarcastic.

"Yeah, I am."

"Welcome to the family, Cap." He extends his hand to me, and I shake it.

"Thanks. Can you keep this to yourself for a few days?"

"Of course. Congrats! My sister may get on my nerves and push me as hard as a mother would, but she's the best." Landry leaves my office.

Relief cascades through me. I'm not sure why I was so nervous about that. Probably because I thought Landry might say no even in jest. There's only one more aspect to my plan. While I was trying to keep those in the know as few as possible, I enlisted the help of Scarlett and Willa. Both ladies provided me with examples of a ring Carly would love. Thankfully, their ideas were in line with my choice. The three stone ring has a two-carat oval center stone with half-moon stones set on either side with a platinum band. It will be ready tomorrow. The best part is we are both off this weekend.

The rest of my day passes uneventfully. Before turning in, I message Carly. We text as frequently as possible during shift days. It keeps us connected, and we don't spend a lot of time chatting in the evening. The same time is better spent for both of us... sleeping.

Me: Sweet dreams. Love you.

Carly: Good night. I love you.

When I leave the fire station the next morning. I make a few stops before going home, including the florist, jeweler, and grocery store. Once home, I set up the puzzle box with my ring inside. After a short swim for pure enjoyment, I shower and get started on our meal.

My woman bursts through the front door soon after work. "Babe, I'm home." I love hearing her call this "home" now.

"Hi, beautiful." I greet her and kiss her. "Why don't you change? Dinner is almost ready. Please grab a hoodie. We're eating outside."

She tilts her head in question, probably because it's early December and chilly. "It's fine to stay inside where it's warm."

I shake my head. "Maybe tomorrow." We're eating near the pool. It's kind of heated, but the glass roof will allow us to gaze at the sky.

I pad to the kitchen and plate our meal. Our culinary delight this evening includes chicken parmesan with penne alla vodka and a spring mix salad. I chose it because it's easy and I'm nervous. Not about her answer but about the ramifications of saying yes to my proposal. Her childhood lacked a stable example of love and marriage, whereas mine was like a Norman Rockwell painting. My hope is her successful matchmaking and the ensuing weddings have shown her a long, loving partnership is possible. We're meant to be and can do anything together.

"Can I help?" she offers.

"Please grab the drinks."

Carly follows me outside. "When did you add twinkle lights?"

I shrug. "Today."

She smiles. "I approve."

I chuckle and dig into my meal. We eat in silence, which is abnormal for us. Usually, we discuss our workdays or off day plans.

"Are you feeling all right?"

"Overall, yeah. I'm just tired. Plus, I'm...." She takes off into the house.

I follow immediately. When I find her, she's hurling in the master en suite. I offer her a washcloth with cool water.

"Thanks."

"Of course."

"How long have you been sick?" I dare ask.

"This is the first time I felt nauseous and vomited, but I've been... exhausted." Her brain is spinning. "Oh. Can you get me my phone?"

I frown but retrieve it from the island. We have a "no phone" policy for three hours each night. It allows us to decompress, talk, and be free from potential work issues. Why does she need it right now? No idea. She's a nurse. It isn't as if she needs to google her....

"Sweetheart?"

She looks from her phone to me and back. When she meets my gaze again, a tear streaks down her cheek. "I'm late."

Warmth blooms in my chest. I wipe her tear and wrap myself around her on the heated tile floor. "You don't seem happy about the possibility of having my child."

She buries her head against my chest and mumbles, "I wanted to be your wife first."

Joy bubbles in my heart. *Glad we agree.* "Do you trust me?"

Carly looks up at me and wrinkles her nose. "Without a doubt."

"Up for a walk?" I don't want to wait any longer to make our dream come true.

She frowns but answers, "Sure." Carly grabs a clean hoodie before we leave the bedroom.

Linking our fingers, I lead her to the set of chairs I built for her. We placed them on the knoll, near the rear of our property. Earlier today, I added a new propane firepit and strung lights in the trees.

About a hundred yards away, a path of rose petals begins, and there's a bouquet of red roses on the small table.

"Alden." My whispered name sounds like a wish and a prayer at once.

I guide her into a chair and start the firepit. Warmth wafts toward her almost instantly. I lift the small puzzle box and hand it to her. It's rectangular with different types of inlaid wood to form her initials. The fact is, when she becomes my wife, her monogram will remain the same.

"It's stunning. You made this?" she asks with awe on her face.

"Yes. Open it." It takes patience for me to watch her figure out the correct order to slide the panels and unveil the Victorian key and hidden lock.

She lifts the lid, revealing a blue velvet box. I shift in front of her on one knee.

"For years, I closed myself off from a second chance on love. With a nudge from a well-meaning mother and brother, my eyes were opened to the possibility of happiness. Your love and trust makes me a better man. Carly, will you take my name and build a family with me?"

"Yes. Absolutely yes!" She throws her arms around my neck with the box trapped between us. Before sealing the deal with a toe-curling, epic kiss, I retrieve the ring box. Taking her hand in mine, I slide my ring on her finger and kiss above it. "I love you, future Mrs. Rhodes."

"I love you."

I meet her mouth and kiss her until the wind picks up.

"Why don't we finish this celebration inside? I would offer dessert, but I'm not sure that's wise."

My gorgeous fiancée smiles. "You can eat it. I'm going to hold off."

I rise and kiss the top of her head. After shutting off the lights and the firepit, we walk home.

"How long can we keep this to ourselves?"

I look over and grin at her. "Our engagement... a few days at most. Our child... depends on how you're feeling."

She smiles. "We're going to be a family."

"We are." Our future is together, and I'm excited for every possibility to begin.

EPILOGUE

GLADYS

At first, the prospect of my book club ending was upsetting. My emotions are more mixed now. I didn't start pairing my coworkers and friends with the intention of finding a wife for my son. Although, both of those things happened.

I call the room to order for the final meeting of the Matchmakers' Book Club.

"Are you ready for this?" Carly asks.

"It's time, dear."

She smiles and steps to the edge of the room beside her future husband, who happens to be my son. I'm grateful my small subterfuge with Carly's brother forced them to see what I saw so many years ago. They're a perfect match.

"Good evening. Thank you for coming. I'm happy to welcome you to our first and last Matchmaker meeting of the book club." Every couple brought together by our meddling received an invitation for this evening. "Each pair in this room was brought together by innocent meddling on the part of your friends and coworkers. Perhaps it was assigning you to boys' games instead of girls' for extra duty." I look pointedly at Captain William Ramirez, who scheduled Callan Craven to monitor the boys' basketball games where he met his wife, Alannah and her son, Caden. "Or you offered assistance to a fellow first responder by providing the name of an ambitious nursing student to care for his ailing mother." Willa Capelli did exactly that for Zack and Scarlett Smithson. "Nearly all of you were completely unaware of the meddling until you had already fallen in love. Recently, the group has received pushback and requests for removal from our honoree list. Carly and I have decided to end the matchmaking portion of our book club. We will continue to support the local first responder community charity endeavors and book discussion."

"Can we open it to guys who read as well?" Zack Smithson asks.

A few other gentlemen in attendance agree with his request.

Carly replies, "I don't see why not."

The guys hoot and holler.

I raise my hand to quiet the chatter. "Over the last seven years, this group has fostered seven couples, beginning with Micah and Jodi Mitchell and culminating with Alden Rhodes and Carly Reed. Please enjoy the refreshments and vote for our next book selection on your way out."

The group claps. I exhale slowly and watch the happy couples chat. A sense of pride washes over me. I fostered these families with a little help from my girl gang. I'm grateful for the chance to do so.

"Thank you, Gladys," Carly states when I join her and my son off to the side of the room.

"Pairing you two was the easiest match of my tenure. At the outset of the book club, I always had Alden in the back of my mind. It wasn't until I met you that his partner became evident. The rest was patience and timing."

Carly and Alden hug me and mingle amongst the guests. As I watch these couples, I reminisce on the joy it brought me to foster them and their happiness into our community and the future.

Thank you so much for reading!

Did you love *For Love & Invisible String?*

Thank you for taking the time to read it. I hope you loved it!
If you liked this book or another one of my books, please consider posting a review.
A short line or two will be perfect! It helps indie authors like me get noticed. I appreciate your support and feedback.

COMING SOON

A Soren Family Novel

MY BOOKS

Protecting Us

Hers to Protect

Protecting our Family

Protecting Home

Agent Protection

MATCHMAKERS' BOOK CLUB

For Love & Coffee

For Love & Basketball

For Love & Cookies

For Love & Photos

SCALA TALENT & SPORTS MANAGEMENT

Moonshot

Our Messy Sequel

THE SOREN FAMILY

Unexpected Forever

All my books in one place: www.nicolevidal.com/books